"I'm betting we don't make it to the sofa," Dino said

Cat didn't reply because it was taking all her concentration to lower his zipper. Biting hard on her lower lip, she started to drag down the snug-fitting jeans.

"Wait."

Stilling her hands, she glanced up in time to see him dig into his back pocket and drop a few condoms onto the table.

"There are three," he said. "Since I go with my feelings, I like to be prepared."

Cat sank to her knees and refocused her attention on tugging his jeans down his legs. Beneath them, he wore a pair of black briefs, stretched almost sheer, which clearly revealed the size of his erection. Licking her suddenly dry lips, she said, "It's like a present."

Dino groaned as Cat traced a finger down the length of him. "Consider it yours. *Please.*"

Dear Reader,

Writing *Come Toy with Me* has given me a chance to return to the Angelis family one last time and tell Dino's story. You may remember his cousins Kit, Nik and Theo, from the TALL, DARK...AND DANGEROUSLY HOT! trilogy I wrote for Harlequin Blaze in 2007. And Dino's cousin Philly recently met her match in my August 2008 Blaze novel *Lie with Me*.

When his admiral asks for a favor, navy captain Dino Angelis postpones his plans to visit his family for Christmas and agrees to take on a special assignment—act the role of fiancé to his admiral's godchild, Cat McGuire, and investigate the smuggling that's going on in her toy store. The job is complicated by two things: Dino's intense attraction to Cat and his gut feeling—the one that served him well when he was working special ops—that Cat is in mortal danger.

A fake fiancé is the last thing Cat needs for Christmas— especially when the man is tall, dark and drop-dead gorgeous! Doesn't she have enough on her mind—a store packed with last-minute Christmas shoppers and a delayed shipment of dolls from Mexico? But once Dino Angelis walks into her life, she can't stop thinking about him—or about getting him out of his uniform.

I hope you enjoy reading Dino and Cat's story as much as I've enjoyed writing it. And please visit my Web site for news about upcoming releases, articles on writing, recipes and more: www.carasummers.com.

Happy holidays!

Cara Summers

COME TOY WITH ME
Cara Summers

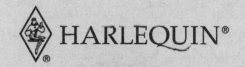

HARLEQUIN®

TORONTO • NEW YORK • LONDON
AMSTERDAM • PARIS • SYDNEY • HAMBURG
STOCKHOLM • ATHENS • TOKYO • MILAN • MADRID
PRAGUE • WARSAW • BUDAPEST • AUCKLAND

Recycling programs
for this product may
not exist in your area.

ISBN-13: 978-0-373-79441-6
ISBN-10:   0-373-79441-X

COME TOY WITH ME

Copyright © 2008 by Carolyn Hanlon.

This is a work of fiction. Names, characters, places and incidents are either the product of the author's imagination or are used fictitiously, and any resemblance to actual persons, living or dead, business establishments, events or locales is entirely coincidental.

This edition published by arrangement with Harlequin Books S.A.

www.eHarlequin.com

Printed in U.S.A.

ABOUT THE AUTHOR

Cara Summers has written more than thirty stories for Harlequin Books, and this year she has been awarded the *Romantic Times BOOKreviews* Career Achievement Award for Series Storyteller of the Year. *Come Toy with Me* is her fifteenth Harlequin Blaze novel, and she's looking forward to writing many more. Her next project for Blaze will be a two-book WRONG BED miniseries, involving identical twin sisters. Look for it in June and July, 2009. When Cara isn't writing books, she teaches in the writing program at Syracuse University.

To my sister Janet—my biggest fan and supporter.
I love you and I wish you all the best as you begin
a new chapter in your life.
You go, girl!

1

"IF YOU HAVE PLANS for Christmas, cancel them."

Retired Colonel James McGuire fired the order at him the moment Dino Angelis strolled into the office on the top floor of the Merceri Bank Building. Dino took his time walking across the expanse of Oriental carpet as he studied the tall, gruff-spoken man standing behind the carved oak desk.

Admiral Robert Maxwell, Dino's boss, had described his oldest and dearest friend accurately. James McGuire was a tall, lean man in his early sixties who despite his white hair appeared to be several years younger. McGuire had retired from the army two years previously and married his second wife, Gianna Merceri, who would one day inherit the Merceri banking fortune. Since then he'd worked as a VP for the New York City branch. Though he was wearing an impeccably tailored business suit, the colonel's bearing and tone of command marked him unmistakably as ex-military.

"Much as I hate to ruin anyone's holiday, this job may take longer than either one of us would like," McGuire continued.

Dino sighed inwardly. Okay, so his hunch that he wouldn't make it home for Christmas had been right. Ninety percent of the time what his family referred to as his premonitions were extremely accurate. They'd saved his life on more than one occasion. But this would make three Christmases in a row he hadn't been with his family, and his cousin Theo was getting married on December 27th.

Not for the first time, Dino asked himself if there'd been some way of getting out of this assignment that he'd overlooked. But Admiral Maxwell owed Colonel McGuire a favor, and Dino owed his admiral, big-time. For the last two years he'd worked in special operations under Maxwell's command. Three months ago, he'd been shot on one of his missions. A bullet had come within an inch of his spine. Recuperating in hospitals in Germany and later in D.C. had given him time to reevaluate how he wanted to spend the rest of his life. He'd joined the navy because he loved the sea. He'd wanted adventure and to see the world. Plus, he'd sensed it was what he was supposed to do. Now, he wanted a job that wouldn't isolate him so completely from his cousins, his uncle and his mother. He missed the closeness, the connectedness he always found with his family. Admiral Maxwell had not only understood his decision, but he'd worked hard to expedite Dino's discharge, and Dino liked to repay his debts.

So he had committed to do a job that he knew nothing about—except that it involved McGuire's family. Of course, Maxwell had used that information as part of the bait. He knew that for Dino, family was important, given it was one of the main reasons he wanted out of the navy. McGuire also knew Dino had expressed an interest in getting into some kind of investigative or security work when he returned to civilian life and that this assignment would be a good opportunity to give it a whirl.

To make the job even more tempting, the admiral had even given Dino the business card of an old navy buddy, Jase Campbell, who was now running his own security firm in Manhattan. Dino had done his first two special ops missions for Maxwell with Jase at his side, and they'd found their styles complementary. Jase was a meticulous planner, and Dino was good at improvising and going with his hunches.

McGuire made a stabbing motion with the unlit cigar he held in his hand. "The truth is this problem I want you to solve for me may stretch into the new year."

Good thing he hadn't promised his mother that he would make it home. Of course Cass Angelis probably already knew not to expect him. Psychic powers ran strong, especially in the women on his mother's side of the family. His mother claimed the psychic abilities could be traced back to the Oracle at Delphi, and hers were particularly powerful.

When he'd been a kid, he'd been hard pressed to get away with anything. She'd always known what he was up to. But his own hunches had kept him out of scrapes on more than one occasion. Recalling that, Dino bit back a smile and refocused his attention on the colonel.

"Perhaps you could tell me exactly what kind of a job you're offering. Admiral Maxwell said that it had something to do with a family problem, but he didn't offer any details."

Maxwell had been apologetic about that. He'd explained that his friend McGuire hadn't been forthcoming. All he'd said was that he'd needed the best man Maxwell could come up with. Dino figured that whether or not he was Maxwell's "best" man was debatable. What couldn't be argued was that he was available. With his discharge papers from the navy due to come through within the next month, he'd just been pushing papers for Maxwell at the Pentagon.

Frowning, the colonel gave Dino a brief nod as he set the cigar down on the desk. "A family problem. I suppose that's one way to describe it. My—"

The intercom on his phone interrupted him and a brisk

female voice spoke. "Colonel, your daughter is returning your call. She's on line three."

"Thank you, Margie." As he reached for the phone, McGuire met Dino's eyes. "I have to take this."

Taking advantage of the opportunity, Dino glanced around the room, absorbing the details. The wall behind him was made of glass and offered a view of the waiting area—a one-way view that allowed Colonel McGuire to see anyone who stepped into the lobby. He wondered how long the colonel had been studying him while he'd been cooling his heels in the lobby.

Through the wall-to-wall window behind McGuire, Dino could see a wintry view of Central Park. The trees were bare of leaves, the ground a dismal brownish-gray, and a serious snowstorm was promised tomorrow. Over a foot of snow was being predicted and Manhattanites were looking forward to a white Christmas. Now that it was almost certain that he was going to be in the Big Apple for the holiday season, Dino was looking forward to it, too. San Francisco had never offered much in the way of white Christmases.

Bookshelves lined the wall to his right, and a large portrait of a woman graced the wall to his left. The brass plaque beneath the painting read: Lucia Merceri. Admiral Maxwell had mentioned her, describing her as the grand matriarch of the Merceri family, a woman with a will of iron. Though she lived in a villa outside of Rome, Lucia kept close track of her family members in New York. In the painting, she wore a black suit, her white hair was pulled up into a ballerina's knot, and she carried a walking cane in her right hand. But it was the dark, piercing eyes that captured Dino's attention. This was a woman who took no prisoners.

"Cat, darling, I need to see you today. How about lunch?"

At the abrupt change in the colonel's tone, Dino shifted his gaze back to him and was struck by how much his stern expression had softened.

"I know how busy you are. A toy store at Christmas—it must be total chaos. But don't you need a break? I thought I might lure you out to that place on Forty-fifth Street you like so much. You have to eat."

Dino knew that Cat McGuire was the colonel's only child by a first marriage. According to Admiral Maxwell, Nancy McGuire had died of MS when Cat was ten, and during the next eight years until Cat had entered college, the colonel had made sure that his daughter had been with him on every assignment barring those that took him directly into combat zones. Even then, McGuire had tried to station his daughter in a place where he could visit her as frequently as possible.

"A delivery?" Disappointment laced the colonel's tone. "I know there are only five shopping days left until Christmas—yes, right, four and a half. But can't one of your employees sign for it?"

The almost wheedling note in the colonel's voice surprised Dino. This man was a sharp right turn from the one who'd fired orders at him a few minutes ago. McGuire chose that moment to glance at him and wave him into a chair. It was only then that Dino realized he'd been standing at attention ever since he'd stopped in front of the desk.

But Cat McGuire evidently didn't take orders from her father. In fact, she seemed to be doing most of the talking.

Intrigued, Dino settled himself in a comfortable leather chair and stretched out his legs. His admiral's close relationship with McGuire could be traced back to the fact that they'd grown up together in Toledo, Ohio, and graduated from the same high school. Though one had gone to Annapolis and the other to West Point, their friendship had never faded. Maxwell was even Cat's godfather.

The admiral had shown him a framed photo of his god-daughter. The moment he'd glanced at it, Dino had experienced a heightening of his senses and he'd known the same way he supposed his mother knew things that the Fates were offering him something he shouldn't walk away from.

It had been the same when he'd been working special ops under Admiral Maxwell. He'd always sensed which ones to volunteer for. The danger that had lain in wait for him on his last mission had come to him in a vision. On the rare occasions that he experienced one, the image always flashed into his mind like the negative of a black-and-white photo. His pre-knowledge had probably saved his life.

When he'd been looking at Cat's picture, he'd also experienced a very strong attraction. He'd tried to rationalize it. After all, it had been a long time since he'd had a woman in his life. The kind of work he'd been doing for the past two years hadn't left time for anything personal. And she was definitely pretty with long red-blond hair and fair skin. The hint of cheekbones suggested strength and the set of her chin spoke of stubbornness.

But it was her eyes that he'd stared at the longest. They were oval-shaped and in the photo they were a glorious mix of gold and green. Cat's eyes. A man could get lost in them.

Warning bells had sounded in his mind. He was starting a new phase of his life. He wanted more contact with his family, and he needed to find out if the skills he'd been honing in the navy could be translated into a career in the private sector. That was a lot for a man to have on his plate.

It was the wrong time to become involved with a woman—especially one who pulled him the way Cat McGuire did.

Colonel McGuire picked up the cigar again and tapped it on the desk. "If lunch is out, let's meet for drinks once you close up shop…eight o'clock? I thought you closed at seven."

There was a pause, then the colonel continued, "Eight it is. How about meeting me midtown at the bar in the Algonquin?"

The cigar tapped in a faster rhythm. "All right, Patty's Pub it is—right across from your store. Eight o'clock."

When he hung up the phone, McGuire sank into his chair and sent Dino an exasperated look. "Ninety percent of the people I negotiate with are easier to manage than she is. I swear she lives and breathes that store."

"The Cheshire Cat."

"Yes. *Alice in Wonderland* was her favorite book when she was little." Setting down his unlit and unsmoked cigar, he narrowed his eyes on Dino. "Did my friend Maxwell fill you in on the name of the store?"

"No. I looked it up myself." He'd been curious about it, as well as its owner, so he'd paid it a visit early that morning. Merely as a little reconnaissance mission, he'd told himself. The more you knew before you took on a job, the better.

The Cheshire Cat hadn't opened yet, but he'd checked out the display windows and found himself charmed by the thematic way the toys were arranged in each one. One told a story of pirates, and the other featured a battle between a dragon and a valiant knight.

Then beyond the artfully arranged toys his attention had been caught by Cat McGuire hurrying down a wrought iron spiral staircase in the center of the store. Once she reached the bottom, she'd flown to the door and pulled it open.

Dino had experienced an even greater heightening of his senses than he'd felt when he'd looked at her photo. And no wonder. She'd been pretty enough in the picture, but in person, she was stunning. And tall. In the boots she was wearing, she had to be nearly five ten.

Though Dino had known he was staring, he couldn't seem to stop. She'd fastened her hair back from her face with some feminine bit of magic, and red-gold curls had tumbled to her shoulders. He'd wondered if they would feel warm to the touch. Silver hoops had hung from her ears, and the dark blue sweater she'd worn belted over a long flowing skirt had him thinking fancifully of gypsies dancing in the firelight.

As customers filed into the Cheshire Cat, her gaze had met his—for just an instant. He'd felt the impact like a swift, hard punch in the gut. Then his mind had emptied and all he'd been aware of was her eyes. He'd read the same startled response in them that he was feeling—a reckless, nearly overpowering desire. Then the green had darkened to the color of the Mediterranean Sea at twilight, completely alluring. What color would those eyes turn when a man made love to her? When he was inside of her?

Before he could get a handle on his thoughts, an image had flashed into his mind—he and Cat standing against a wall. Except for a few wispy pieces of lace she was naked, her bare legs wrapped around him. And he was thrusting into her, pulling out, thrusting in again.

Recalling it now, his whole body hardened, his blood heated.

"I checked you out, too," McGuire was saying.

Dino ruthlessly reined in his thoughts. But he had less luck controlling his body's reaction to the image fading from his mind.

"I don't mind telling you that I specifically asked Bobby to find me an army man."

Dino met McGuire's eyes steadily. "Admiral Maxwell told me to tell you that with a navy man you're trading up."

McGuire grinned, then broke into a full belly laugh. The sound filled the room, and Dino felt the corners of his mouth curve.

"That sounds like Bobby," McGuire said. Then his expression sobered. "I trust Bobby to have chosen the right man, and that means I trust you with my daughter's safety."

Dino once more felt that heightening of his senses. Hadn't he known from the beginning that the job would be about the daughter? Wasn't that precisely why he'd gone to the store to check her out? And considering his intense reaction to Cat as a woman, he was going to have to be very careful.

"Why don't you tell me exactly what it is that you want me to do?"

The colonel met Dino's eyes directly. "You already know that my daughter Cat owns and runs a toy store in Tribeca. She's been doing it for a year and a half now. Before that, she was in the toy department at Macy's and worked her way up to head buyer."

McGuire picked up his cigar yet again, but still made no move to light it. "The fact that Cat's in retail is a problem for my wife's family, especially for my mother-in-law, Lucia Mercuri."

McGuire gestured to the portrait that Dino had studied earlier. "That woman is a true matriarch. She runs her family with the verve and determination of a five-star general. When Cat met her at Gianna's and my wedding, she likened her to the Queen of Hearts in *Alice in Wonderland.*"

Dino was beginning to wonder where McGuire was headed.

"Ever since we married, Lucia has been pressuring my wife, Gianna, to find a suitable husband for Cat so that she can take her rightful place in New York City society. Lucia believes that women have a duty to produce a family, to contribute to the community, and that they should leave the business world to men. Unfortunately, she's influenced my wife's thinking in that direction, too."

"I take it Cat disagrees."

"That's putting it mildly. But between us, we can usually handle Gianna."

Dino frowned. "Does this job have something to do with running interference between your wife and your daughter? Because if—"

"No." McGuire raised a hand, palm outward. "I can handle that part myself. I'm getting to be quite good at it although at times it's a little like moving through a minefield. The trouble my daughter is in has to do with that shop of hers."

Dino merely raised his brows.

"The Cheshire Cat imports and sells unique toys. There's nothing in the place that you would find in one of the big chain stores or even in the more upscale department stores. Almost everything is one of a kind. About a year ago when Cat was still doing a lot of traveling, she discovered a town in Mexico, Paxco, where doll- and toy-making are highly revered and a local cottage industry. She signed a contract with the craftsmen, and in the past year, has imported a number of products from Paxco.

Dino said nothing. For the first time since he'd walked into the office, he heard worry in the colonel's voice.

McGuire picked up his cigar and jabbed it at the air again. "That's where the trouble is. Someone has taken advantage of my little girl."

"How?" Dino asked.

"Some bastard is smuggling drugs into the country in those toys. Cocaine."

Dino thought for a minute. How much cocaine could be smuggled in toys? "It must be a rather small-scale operation."

McGuire's expression turned very grim. "Small, but very profitable. My contacts at the CIA tell me that the cocaine is premium quality and the person running the operation targets a select group of clients who are willing to pay very generously for high quality and the guaranteed discretion of the distributor."

Dino nodded thoughtfully. "The rich folks don't have to lower themselves to rubbing elbows with someone on the street."

"Exactly. But drugs aren't the worst of it. The profits from this little enterprise are being used by a terrorist group out of Latin America to help establish a cell in this country. That's brought in both Homeland Security and the feds—which means the whole situation's got cluster fuck written all over it."

Dino silently agreed. "Does your daughter know about the smuggling?"

The colonel shook his head. "I thought about telling her, but I know her too well. She'd be furious that someone was using her shop that way. There's no way I could convince her to keep her nose out of it. She'd start poking around, and that could put her in even more danger."

"What else did your CIA informants tell you about the operation?"

"Someone on the other end in one of those small towns is loading the drugs into the toys just before they're shipped here."

Simple, safe, Dino thought. And a toy store was a good cover. "There has to be someone in the store who knows which pieces have the drugs in them."

"Yes." McGuire tapped his cigar on the desk. "And the feds' prime suspect is my daughter. They think she's part of a damn terrorist smuggling ring."

Dino kept his eyes steady. "Is she?"

McGuire's color heightened, but there was no other sign of his brief struggle for control. His voice was flat and firm when he spoke. "No. She's not. From the time she was a little girl, she's dreamed of running a toy shop—a place where she could make children's dreams come true. That was her mother's dream, too. Nancy even designed some dolls. It was something they shared before Nancy passed. Cat's not involved in this criminal enterprise, but someone else in that shop has to be."

"Any idea who?"

"She has two full-time employees. Her assistant manager is Adelaide Creed, a retired accountant, and Cat looks on her as a second mother. And she often speaks of her buyer, Matt Winslow, as the brother she never had. She also has a part-time employee, Josie Sullivan, a sixty-five-year-old retired schoolteacher. Any one of them is close enough to the business to be involved. Hell, they could all be working together."

"I assume you've run background checks on each of them, and none of them has an urgent need for money, or a sudden influx of the same."

McGuire nodded. "I used a man your boss recommended— Jase Campbell. He researched their finances and found nothing out of the ordinary. On top of that they each appear to be stellar citizens. Josie was given an award from the mayor for excellence in teaching, and Matt is going to school at night to get his MBA. When she first retired from her career as an accountant, Adelaide Creed worked for Congresswoman Jessica Atwell. When the governor appointed Atwell Attorney General, Adelaide applied for work at the Cheshire Cat."

"So you have no leads."

"None. And my informants tell me that the feds expect to move on the operation any day. This whole thing is about to come crashing down on Cat's head."

"And my job is to bodyguard her?"

"Not just that. You'll be on the inside. I want you to take a look around and find out who's on the receiving end of the stolen goods. Maybe you can even get a lead on the mastermind behind the whole thing. According to my sources, the feds don't have much of a clue there. Bobby claims you're one of the best operatives he's ever had under his command. He says you have a special kind of sixth sense when it comes to investigations."

Thinking it was better not to comment on that, Dino said, "Isn't the sudden appearance of a bodyguard going to raise the suspicions of whoever is involved?"

Dino watched some of the tension in the older man ease.

"Not if your cover story is good enough. And yours is excellent."

Noting the gleam in the colonel's eyes, Dino had a hunch that he wasn't going to like it.

"You're my daughter's new fiancé."

2

THE FIRST FIVE BEATS of silence that followed his announcement allowed James McGuire a moment to study the young man sitting across from him. Dino Angelis looked perfectly at ease, his elbows resting on the arms of the chair, his legs stretched out and crossed at the ankles. McGuire had seen the same kind of seeming relaxation in jungle cats while they watched their prey. And like those cats, he wagered that Dino Angelis could move quickly enough when he was ready.

He agreed with Bobby—Angelis was smart. So far, his questions had been perceptive and to the point, his comments insightful. The man didn't believe in wasting words. For a split second, right after he'd said the word *fiancé,* he'd read surprise in the younger man's eyes. Other than that Angelis hadn't revealed much of anything he was thinking since he'd ambled into the room. He'd make a formidable opponent in a poker game.

As the five beats stretched into ten, McGuire said, "Any questions?"

Dino raised one finger. "Who's going to believe in a fiancé who turns up out of the blue?"

Once again he'd zeroed in on a key point. McGuire opened a drawer in his desk and pulled out a manila envelope. "Got it covered. This is your complete history with my daughter—

from first meet to secret weekends here in Manhattan at the Waldorf to the night that you popped the question on the skating rink at Rockefeller Center. Melted my little girl's heart. She loves to skate—could have competed nationally if we hadn't had to move around so much. Your relationship has been hush-hush so far, but Cat's invited you here for Christmas to publicly announce the engagement and to meet her family. You have a two-week leave from the Pentagon."

"Where am I going to be staying? I can't do a very good job of protecting your daughter if I go back to my hotel room every night."

McGuire opened the envelope and pulled out a key. "Cat's apartment building is a co-op. A few months ago, the apartment next to hers became available, and I bought it for her as a surprise Christmas gift, figuring she could expand the space she has now. You can stay there. Both apartments overlook a courtyard that connects the building to the block the Cheshire Cat is on. As far as Cat's employees are concerned, it will appear that you're staying with her. You'll have a day to memorize your background story before you drop in at the shop and surprise my little girl."

"How is your daughter going to react to all this? Won't she want to know why you've hired me to act as her bodyguard?"

"I'm not going to tell her that part."

"Then why would she agree to this fake fiancé masquerade?"

"I'm going to persuade her to cooperate over drinks this evening."

Dino's eyes narrowed. "You think she'll agree?"

McGuire kept his smile easy, confident. There *was* still that little obstacle to overcome. Cat was her father's daughter. She could be stubborn when she wanted to.

"Cat has a weakness for wanting to please her father—

especially at Christmastime. And the fake engagement is the only way to protect my wife and daughter from Lucia Merceri."

Dino inclined his head toward the portrait on the wall. "I'm not following. What part does your mother-in-law play in all of this?"

"Nothing in the drug smuggling part. But the old battle-ax is the prime mover in the fake engagement scenario." McGuire leaned back in his chair. "Just about the time I learned about the danger my daughter is in, my wife came to me in tears. It seems that over the past year, her mother has been asking for progress reports on what Gianna is doing to get Cat 'settled.' Turns out my wife has been placating her mother with stories, telling her that Cat has been seeing someone secretly. Gianna told Lucia she discovered the trysts by accident and she hasn't wanted to get involved because she was afraid of jinxing it."

"An interesting story," Dino commented.

"Yeah. In my wife's defense, I have to say that she's been focused on her daughter Lucy's pregnancy and didn't have much time left over to run a campaign to get Cat a husband. So she made up a whopper. And Lucia's been fascinated by it. Last week she announced that she was coming over here to celebrate Christmas with us, and she wants to meet the man Cat is seeing. My wife is in a panic about what her mother will do when she discovers the lie. It won't take Cat long to figure out that if she goes along with this masquerade, she can bring some peace to the family during the holidays, and her stepmother will owe her. Christmas is a special time for Cat. She wants to make everyone happy. And Lucia is flying back to Rome on New Year's Day. Crisis over."

Dino studied the colonel. "So the fake engagement is supposed to fool your mother-in-law until New Year's Day?"

"It could actually last a bit beyond that, depending on how the drug smuggling problem is resolved. I'm leaving the story about your eventual breakup in Gianna's capable hands. Apparently my wife can lie like a trouper."

Dino unfolded himself from the chair and picked up the key and the envelope. "If that's all, sir, I'll take this back to my hotel room and go over the specifics."

McGuire rose and extended his hand. "Good, good. You'll report for duty at the Cheshire Cat tomorrow no later than eleven hundred hours."

"Yes, sir."

McGuire waited until Dino had his hand on the doorknob. "One more thing."

Dino glanced back.

"It's not part of the job, but it would be great if you could get Cat to relax and have a little fun. The girl is so focused on her store that she doesn't take time to smell the roses anymore."

"I'll see what I can do."

McGuire managed to hold in his sigh of relief until he'd watched the elevator doors slide shut on Dino Angelis. That had gone almost too smoothly. Then he took his cell phone out of his pocket and dialed a familiar number at the Pentagon.

"Jimmy, you've called to tell me you owe me fifty bucks, right?" Bobby Maxwell asked.

Grinning, McGuire sank into his chair. Bobby had always been a bit cocky, so he kept his tone serious. "You haven't won the bet yet. They haven't even met. And first things first. My daughter's in danger. That's his primary mission."

"A little adventure is just what they need. It'll bring them closer."

"It might turn out to be more than a little adventure."

"Angelis has the best instincts of any man I've ever

trained." Bobby's tone too had turned serious. "If there's something going on in your daughter's store, he'll spot it. And he'll know what to do."

"I hope you're right."

"I am. And I'm also right about the fact that he'd make the perfect man for our little girl."

"We'll see," was all McGuire said. But he was already hoping that his friend Bobby would win the little wager they'd made. He too thought that Dino Angelis just might be the perfect match for Cat.

CASS ANGELIS' CELL PHONE RANG just as she was about to leave the tower room in her house. A glance at the caller ID had joy bubbling up inside of her. "Dino?"

"You probably already know I'm not going to make it home for Christmas."

She'd sensed that much last night. She'd also sensed there was more, but the images she'd seen in her crystals hadn't been clear. Except for the woman—tall with reddish hair and stunning green eyes. Turning, Cass moved to her desk and sat down. The client who was due any minute would have to wait. Cass could hear traffic noises in the background on the other end of the line.

"I'm in Manhattan on a job. I couldn't say no."

"I understand." And Cass did in spite of the band of pain that tightened around her heart.

For a moment, there was silence on the other end of the line, and Cass waited. Of all of her "children," her son Dino had always been the most reserved.

Twelve years ago when her husband Demetrius and her sister Penelope had been killed in a freak boating accident, Cass and Dino, her brother-in-law Spiro and his four children,

Nik, Theo, Kit and Philly, had moved into the huge house Cass's father had built. From that day on, Cass had raised her nephews and niece as her own, and Dino had come to regard them more as brothers and kid sister than cousins. Dino had been the only one who'd had a desire to see the world, the only one who'd moved away from San Francisco.

"There's a woman," Dino finally said. "I sense that the Fates have put her in my path for a reason. And I had a vision about her."

The redhead, Cass knew. "You'll figure it out."

Dino laughed then, and Cass's mood suddenly lightened. "You've been saying that to me for as long as I can remember."

"A mother's job," Cass replied. "And I don't recall that I was ever wrong."

"I'll get home as soon as I possibly can. My discharge papers are coming through in a couple more weeks. That was supposed to be your Christmas present."

"Well." She hadn't seen that, hadn't even allowed herself to hope for it. "I'll have a surprise for you too—when you get here." She wanted Dino to meet Mason Leone, the man she'd been dating, in person before she told him that after all these years, she'd fallen in love again.

The traffic noises grew louder. "I have to go. I'll try to keep in touch. Love you."

"Love you, too," Cass said, but Dino had already disconnected.

A quick glance at her watch told Cass that she still had a few minutes before she had to go down to her office. Crossing quickly to her desk, she took her crystals from a drawer. Midnight was usually the hour when she could see things more clearly. But she simply couldn't wait.

Sinking into her chair, she cleared her mind and waited.

One by one the crystals began to glow in her hands. In their centers, mist blossomed, parted, then closed again. In one, she saw Dino in his full dress uniform dancing with the redheaded woman she'd seen before. Around them, lights twinkled. As the mists thickened in one crystal, they thinned in another.

Cass glimpsed a doll this time, with a porcelain face and a red silk dress. When her attention was drawn to a third crystal, Cass felt fear knot in her stomach. She could see the red-headed woman again, but she was no longer with Dino. She was in a dark place, and she was facing the barrel of a gun. The shot that rang out nearly had Cass dropping her crystals.

In spite of the client who was waiting for her, Cass sat where she was for a few more minutes while fear warred with joy inside of her.

Dino and the woman would be facing serious danger, but Dino had been right. The Fates were making him an offer, and if he chose to accept it, he would find his true love.

ON HER WAY DOWN from her office, Cat took a moment to breathe and glance around her store. A toddler clutching his mother's hand had decided to sing along with the rendition of "Jingle Bells" pouring out of the sound system. Another child was busily plucking ornaments off the Christmas tree she'd set up in one of the corners. Cat grinned. She had to retrim that tree almost every night, but it was worth it.

The bell over the Cheshire Cat's door jingled. From her vantage point halfway up the spiral staircase in the center of her store, Cat spotted Mrs. Lassiter and Mrs. Palmer, two of her most loyal customers. No doubt they were here to pick up their dolls. She dashed down the rest of the stairs. Just as she reached the two women, the bell jingled again, and more customers pushed their way into the store. Cat briefly shifted her gaze to the newcomers, and she immediately recognized them as two sisters, Janey and Angela Carter. They had also ordered the dolls. Cat sent them what she hoped was a welcoming smile.

"I came to pick up my granddaughter's doll," Mrs. Lassiter said in a voice that carried. "It's one of the special ones you ordered from that place in Mexico."

"Yes. From Paxco, Mexico." Cat did her best to project calm reassurance. "I'm sorry, but they haven't arrived yet. I expect them—"

"You said they'd be here today. What's the problem?"

Ignoring the nerves dancing in her stomach, Cat smiled. "No problem."

"When will they arrive?"

Cat wished she knew. "I'm hoping tomorrow. Thursday at the latest."

The bell over the door jingled again, and a portly white-haired man entered and looked around. Cat was sure she'd never seen him before, and yet there was something about him that was familiar. He crossed to Adelaide and cut rudely into the line in front of her counter. Someone voiced a protest, and for a moment Adelaide lost her usual pleasant expression. She even dropped a toy soldier she was about to ring up. Then she said something to the man and pointed in Cat's direction. As he strode toward her, Cat suddenly figured out why he might look familiar. With his white hair and mustache, and the narrow unframed spectacles that sat nearly on the end of his nose, he reminded Cat a bit of Santa Claus.

Oh, how she wished he were. Where was Santa when you needed him?

"But you're not sure?"

Cat shifted her gaze back to Mrs. Lassiter. Worry out-weighed the annoyance in the older woman's voice now, and

Cat could see the same concern reflected in Mrs. Palmer's face, as well as in the Carter sisters'.

The shop was packed. It was Christmas week in Manhattan *and* lunch hour—that time of day when both locals and tourists poured into stores with one purpose—to finish their Christmas shopping.

And her father had wanted her to join him for lunch in midtown? Right. Her family didn't really have a clue about the kind of pressures that built once you combined Christmas, children and toys.

Cat met the worried gazes in front of her one at a time. "I'm confident that the dolls will arrive in the next two days." They had to.

Out of the corner of her eye, she saw that her assistant Adelaide had fully recovered from her encounter with the Santa Claus man and was ringing up a fairly hefty sale for a young couple. Tourists. The man had a camera slung over his shoulder and the woman was unfolding a street map.

"So the bottom line is that you have no idea whether or not the doll I ordered will arrive by Christmas Eve." This time it wasn't Mrs. Lassiter who spoke. It was the Santa Claus man. His voice carried and several customers who'd been browsing nearby stopped to stare in his direction.

"You said the dolls would be here no later than today," Mrs. Lassiter chimed in. "Don't we have a free trade agreement with Mexico? Would it help if I called my congressman?"

Cat turned the full wattage of her smile on the small group gathered in front of her and kept her voice calm. "I don't think it's time to panic yet. I only learned yesterday afternoon that the delivery of the dolls might be delayed a day or so. *Might* be. They could be on their way right now. Each doll is hand-made, and a few of them weren't quite ready for shipment. I told them to ship the ones that were immediately." What she didn't add was that Juan Rivero, who'd called her with the bad news, had answered her by saying that they only needed one more day. And then he'd hung up.

"In the meantime, my buying assistant, Matt Winslow, flew to Paxco, Mexico, late last night. I'm hoping to hear from him any time now."

She should have heard from him already, even with the time difference. And Matt wasn't answering his cell. Cat concentrated on the unhappy faces in front of her and firmly pushed that worry out of her mind.

"Worst case scenario, they'll express ship the ones that are ready today, and Matt will personally bring back the dolls that are holding up the shipment with him."

"You're sure?" This question came from a very worried Mrs. Palmer.

"My granddaughter Giselle is expecting Santa to bring her that doll for Christmas. I showed her your brochure and that doll is the only one she wanted," Mrs. Lassiter said. "I don't want her to be disappointed."

"It's the same with my daughter." In contrast to Mrs. Lassiter's confrontational expression, Mrs. Palmer's eyes held a great deal of worry and sadness. Her black wool coat was off the rack and was growing threadbare at the sleeves. "That doll was the only gift Mandy asked Santa for."

Cat's heart twisted. Both Mrs. Lassiter and Mrs. Palmer frequented her store. And because she made it a habit to learn as much as she could about her customers, Cat was aware of the number of visits that Mrs. Palmer and Mandy had made to the Cheshire Cat to choose that one special gift. If it didn't arrive, Cat wagered there would be nothing else under the tree.

But the shipment *would* arrive. She'd been chanting that

sentence to herself like a mantra all day long. The unique dolls that were now being finshed in the small town of Paxco, Mexico, were even more special to Cat because she'd asked the craftsmen to create them from a design of her mother's. She'd taken twenty-four orders and added on one she intended to give her father. That had been in mid-November.

"The dolls are going to get here," Cat assured the group in front of her. Her gaze lingered on the Santa Claus man. With his index finger, he shoved his glasses to the bridge of his nose and met her gaze for a moment. Once again, something tugged at the edge of her mind. She knew that she'd never seen him in the store and she wondered who had taken his order.

"You can track the shipment, can't you?" The question came from the Santa Claus man in a calm voice.

Cat beamed a smile at him. "Absolutely. Just as soon as I get a tracking number." Matt was supposed to phone her with that information. "Tell you what. I have a list of all your names and your phone numbers. I'll call you just as soon as I get some news from my assistant. It should be before the end of the day. First thing in the morning at the latest."

In her peripheral vision she saw that Adelaide had stepped away from the counter to assist a customer, and there was now a line at the checkout station. Matt was supposed to be here working today, but though she needed him badly, she needed him in Paxco more.

She masked her relief as the small crowd in front of her began to drift away—all except for the Santa Claus man who stepped forward and handed her a card.

"I'd appreciate a call the moment you get the tracking number."

She glanced down at it, noted the ritzy address on East 70th and the name. George Miller. It didn't ring a bell. She glanced back up at him. "Have we met before, Mr. Miller? You look familiar to me, but I can't quite place it."

He gave her a smile that didn't quite reach his eyes. "No. I would have remembered if we'd met before, Ms. McGuire." He turned to exit the shop.

Cat tucked the card into her pocket, took out the notebook she always carried with her, and jotted down a reminder to personally call each customer who was waiting for a doll just as soon as they arrived.

One crisis postponed, she told herself as she moved as quickly as she could toward the checkout counter. As she did, she brushed by Adelaide.

Pitching her voice low, Adelaide said, "Nicely done. You're better than anyone I know at defusing panic attacks."

"I didn't do so well on my own," Cat murmured.

Adelaide shot her a quick sideways glance. "At least no one brought up the Nor'easter that's due to arrive tomorrow. If they close down the airports…"

Cat clamped her hands over her ears, and Adelaide's rich laugh filled the shop. She was a round, comfortable-looking single woman in her late fifties who combined a love of children with an accounting degree from Sarah Lawrence. In addition, she had a personal warmth that reminded Cat of Paula Deen, one of the most popular chefs on the Food Network. Adelaide had retired early from a lucrative job at Price Waterhouse and referred to her work at the Cheshire Cat as her little mad money job.

Adelaide patted Cat's shoulder. "Just teasing. These winter storms are never as bad as the predictions. It's all hype."

"From your mouth to God's ears," Cat said. Then she added, "The man who cut into your checkout line earlier— George Miller—did you take his order for one of the dolls?"

"No. I've never seen him before. Have you?"

Cat shook her head. "But there's something familiar about him."

Out of the corner of her eye, Cat spotted the beginnings of a protest at the checkout counter. Dashing forward, she beamed a smile at the man who was first in line and rang up the sale. While he was signing the credit card receipt, she pulled her cell phone out and speed-dialed her neighbor.

Josie Sullivan was a retired schoolteacher in her early seventies who'd moved into the apartment below Cat's about a year ago. She had an ethereal air that reminded Cat of one of Tennessee Williams' southern heroines. But beneath her seemingly fragile exterior, Josie had an energy and an iron-willed determination that must have served her well in a third-grade classroom.

It certainly worked when she was steering customers toward a sale. Off and on over the past year, Josie had been filling in at the store during what Cat had dubbed the "crush hours." Since their apartments were in the building that shared a courtyard with the Cheshire Cat, Josie could make it to the store on a moment's notice. All she had to do was exit the back of their building, cross the courtyard and take a shortcut down an alley. The arrangement was working out so well that Cat was going to offer her a more permanent part-time job right after the first of the year.

"Cat, tell me you desperately need me in the store," Josie said the instant she picked up her phone. "I'm simply bored to death."

Cat smiled. "I desperately need you in the store." Then she held out her hand to the harried-looking woman who was next in line at the counter. "Sorry you had to wait. Let me take that for you."

By eight o'clock, Cat's head was aching and her feet were killing her, but she was finally able to lock the front door of her toy store. Even though the Cheshire Cat officially closed at seven, the shop had still been filled with shoppers. During the week before Christmas, one had to go with the flow, but she'd insisted that Josie and Adelaide leave at seven. On Thursday they would close at 6:00 so that they could all attend the big charity ball her stepmother chaired each holiday season.

Cat had bought tickets for all of her employees, hoping to placate her stepmother. Gianna Merceri McGuire was not going to be pleased when Cat arrived without a date in tow.

A date. In the past year and a half, the concept had become foreign to her. The last time she'd gone out with a man she'd still been working at Macy's.

It was then that she once more recalled the stranger who'd been standing at the edge of the small crowd on the sidewalk that morning. He'd been teasing his way into her mind all day. This was the first opportunity she'd had to think about the odd reaction she'd had to him.

No, *odd* wasn't the precise word. She'd never had such an intense reaction to a man in her life. Not even to the men she'd taken as lovers. Cat frowned as she recalled that moment when his eyes had collided with hers. The contact had been as intimate as a touch. She hadn't been able to think or move. All she could do was feel. Desire—raw, primitive, compelling—had filled her. And in that instant, an image had formed in her mind of the two of them naked, their legs tangling as they rolled across a floor.

Which was absolutely ridiculous. He was a complete stranger. She'd barely caught a glimpse of him.

But she had no trouble picturing him now. He'd been big, broad-shouldered and tall. He'd had a strong face, like a warrior. In the black leather bomber jacket and jeans, he'd looked tough. Not her usual type. But that hadn't stopped her from imagining their bodies locked together.

Fisting her hands at her side, Cat pushed the image out of her mind. There had to be a rational explanation for what she'd felt—what she was still feeling. First of all, she hadn't slept much the night before. And he was a man who would stand out in any crowd. Her body had obviously been trying to tell her something. Devoting all her time to making the Cheshire Cat a success had left a void in her life. That had to be it.

She'd better get back into the dating scene. Nothing serious. But some simple, uncomplicated sex held a certain appeal. Pulling her notebook out of her jacket pocket, she jotted a note to herself. *New Year's resolution #1: Start dating again.*

And the plan would have certain benefits. Next year she might have an escort for Gianna's charity ball. Her stepmother wanted her in a serious relationship with a "suitable" man— suitable meaning someone with the proper social standing. Cat wasn't about to walk down the path that Gianna had all mapped out for her, but a date now and then, someone to see a movie with—that would be enjoyable.

Right. Who was she kidding? When she'd looked into that stranger's eyes this morning, going to a movie with him had been the last thing on her mind. She'd thought of sex, raw, wild, incredible.

Tucking her notebook back into her pocket, Cat firmly pushed all thoughts of the attractive stranger, the upcoming ball and the questions she would have to handle from her step-mother firmly out of her mind. She had much bigger problems.

Those missing dolls. Striding to the small space behind the cash register, she opened a manila folder and thumbed through the orders she'd removed from her files earlier in the day.

Twenty-four children were going to be disappointed if Matt Winslow didn't get the shipment out of Paxco. And right now twenty-four unhappy customers were waiting to hear from her—and she didn't have any news to give them. Closing the folder, she tucked it into her tote bag.

She hadn't been able to get through to Matt all day, and he hadn't answered any of the messages she'd left on his voice mail. She also hadn't been able to contact Juan Rivero, the man who'd called her yesterday to tell her the shipment of dolls might be delayed.

Taking out her cell, Cat punched in Matt's number again. Listening to the rings, she paced back to the window and scanned the street for her FedEx man. There was still a chance…. But the only truck she spotted was delivering soft drinks to the bar across the street.

Cat closed her eyes and swore under her breath. The *same* bar where she was supposed to be meeting her father right now! Whirling, she dashed back to the counter and grabbed her tote. She was about to close her cell, when she heard the faint voice in her ear.

"Cat?"

She raced to the second step of the spiral staircase where reception for her cell was usually clearest.

"Matt, where are you? Tell me you've shipped the dolls."

The only reply she received was a burst of static.

"Matt? Are you there?"

"Bad…"

"What?" Please not bad news, Cat prayed.

"Connection…terrible."

He was right about that. His voice was fading in and out. Cat bit back on her impulse to ask him why he hadn't called all day. Only one thing mattered now. "Tell me you shipped the dolls."

"…tomorrow…Thursday…"

There was another burst of static. Which was it? Did he mean that they wouldn't ship until tomorrow? Or that they would arrive tomorrow? Thursday was two days from now. Cat swallowed her disappointment. Starting tomorrow afternoon, there could be delays because of that Nor'easter moving up the coast.

"…want to be there…to open them. Need to…"

"Did you ship all of them?"

There was another burst of static and then the connection was broken. Cat punched in Matt's number again, but this time she was transferred to his voice mail.

"Call me back with the tracking number," she said.

She'd feel better once she had something more concrete to go on.

In the meantime, her father was waiting, and tardiness had always been an issue with him. She set the security alarm, locked the door behind her, dashed toward the curb and quickly threaded her way through traffic to Patty's Pub. Through the window, she spotted her father already seated at one of the tables.

For the first time all day, she had time to wonder just what urgent matter had brought her father all the way down to this end of town.

THE PHONE RANG, and the hand that reached for the receiver trembled slightly. *Breathe. Don't panic.* "Hello."

"Where are the dolls?" The voice on the other end of the line was soft and chilling.

A shudder was ruthlessly suppressed. "They've been delayed. They should arrive tomorrow—Thursday at the latest."

The long silence caused a fresh flutter of panic.

"You'll be in the shop when the shipment arrives?"

"Yes. Of course."

"I'll expect the doll I ordered no later than Thursday. Otherwise..."

The line went dead.

3

JAMES MCGUIRE ROSE as his daughter threaded her way through the packed restaurant. The crowd was a lively one, and the noise level nearly succeeded in muting the tinny-sounding Christmas carols that poured through the speakers. He'd arrived half an hour early and tipped the hostess to find him a table.

This wasn't the type of place he would have chosen, but he'd learned years ago to pick his battles with his daughter. And a pretty little waitress named Colleen had informed him that the Mulligan's stew here had been written up in the *Zagat's* guide.

A rush of love moved through him when Cat wrapped her arms around him in a warm hug. When he drew back, he held on to her for a moment and studied her face. Just as he'd suspected, there were circles under her eyes. Even as a child, she'd always given every project she worked on her all. It was high time she had something in her life besides that toy store. "It's been too long, little girl. You have to get away from that store sometimes. I miss you."

"You could always come down to this end of town and visit me in the Cheshire Cat," she said.

McGuire winced a little. "Touché. One guilt trip deserves another. Sit down. I ordered you a glass of your favorite wine. Pouilly-Fuissé, right?"

"Right."

"Colleen here recommended the Mulligan's stew, so I took the liberty of ordering that, too. I'll bet you didn't take time for lunch today."

Cat narrowed her eyes on her father. "You want something. Why don't you just come out with it?"

"Now, Cat, can't you believe your dad just wanted to see you?"

Her eyes narrowed even more. "Maybe when pigs fly."

He threw back his head and laughed. "Never could put one over on you, could I?"

"Maybe when I was six."

He raised his glass. "At least take a sip of that wine. It costs the earth."

Cat's brows shot up as she reached for her wine. "And that single malt Scotch you're drinking doesn't?"

He merely smiled as he touched his glass to hers. "To a very happy holiday season."

Cat sipped her wine. "You've got that gleam in your eyes. You're up to something. If you came all the way down here to make sure I'm going to Gianna's big charity ball on Thursday, I'll be there. I also bought tickets for Adelaide, Josie and Matt. He should be back from Mexico by then."

"Mexico?" He had to tread carefully. He wasn't supposed to know much about her store.

She smiled as she took another sip of wine. "He's in this little village. I've told you about Paxco, haven't I?"

"Remind me," he said. She actually started to glow when she talked about her business. It was something she rarely spoke of when the family gathered because of Gianna's preference that she get out of retail. His wife had even gone so far as to offer her a job at Merceri Bank.

"Matt had to fly down there yesterday because this one shipment of dolls has been delayed. If it doesn't get here, there are going to be twenty-four little girls who won't get what they want from Santa."

No wonder she was worried, McGuire thought. Her mother had died on Christmas Eve, and ever since then, Cat had put a lot of effort into making sure that everything was perfect at Christmastime. He'd done the same for her. But he couldn't read any sign that she suspected something other than doll-making was going on in Paxco. He placed a hand over hers. "Don't worry, little girl. They'll get here."

She lifted her chin. "I know that, and that's exactly what I told my worried customers. I'm hoping they shipped today and they'll arrive tomorrow or Thursday. Friday at the latest."

She sipped more wine. "Still, I'll feel better when Matt calls back and gives me a tracking number. The connection I had with him was very bad."

McGuire studied his daughter. He didn't like it one bit that one of the shipments from Paxco was delayed. If something happened to prevent the drugs from arriving, or even worse, if someone at the other end had gotten greedy, it might very well increase the danger to Cat.

Thank heavens, Dino Angelis would be at her side beginning tomorrow morning.

"About Gianna's ball…"

Cat met his eyes. "I told you I'll be there."

"But you don't have a date."

"And just how do you know that?"

Hearing the thread of annoyance in her tone, he took a drink of his Scotch. "A smart army man never reveals his sources."

Cat regarded him steadily as she took another taste of wine.

"All I want is a favor. I'd look upon it as your Christmas

gift to me. And you can check Gianna off your list at the same time. I'm offering you a two-for-the-price-of-one deal."

She still said nothing. McGuire wondered not for the first time why she couldn't have taken more after Nancy than him.

"C'mon, Cat. Your daddy shouldn't have to beg."

Cat threw up both of her hands. "Okay. I'm not agreeing to anything yet. Just what is it that you want me to do?"

"Just get engaged for Christmas."

CAT STARED at her father. She sincerely hoped that her mouth hadn't dropped open because she knew that was just the reaction he was hoping for. Her mom and dad had always played chess together, and after her mother had died, she'd asked her father to teach her the game. But even after she'd joined the chess team at school, she'd never been able to beat him. He was a master strategist. Just what was he up to?

"You're joking."

"I couldn't be more serious."

She glanced at his drink. "How many of those did you have while you were waiting for me?"

He shook his head sadly. "Is that anything for a respectful daughter to ask her father?"

She sipped her wine and leaned back in her chair. "Are you going to tell me what you're up to?"

"Thought you'd never ask. Gianna has gotten herself into a little scrape." He told her the same story he'd told Dino Angelis and watched her eyes widen. Unlike the navy captain, she'd had the experience of meeting Lucia Merceri.

"So the Queen of Hearts is going to arrive tomorrow and catch her daughter in a lie?"

"Unless I solve the problem."

"How?"

"It's simple. I've hired you a fiancé for Christmas."

"You've what?"

Several people in the immediate area sent glances her way, so Cat clamped down on her emotions and hissed, "You've hired me a fiancé? And where, pray tell, did you get him—some kind of escort service?"

Colleen appeared at their table and set down two bowls of Mulligan's stew. "Is there anything else I can get you?"

Cat managed a tight smile. "No." But she would have liked to order a bucket of cold ice water to pour over her father's head.

As if sensing the tension at the table, Colleen's bright smile wavered. "Enjoy your meal." Then she scurried away.

"You've scared that poor little waitress."

Keeping her voice pitched low, Cat leaned forward. "Don't you put that on me. If you don't tell me what you're up to, you may end up wearing what's left of my very expensive wine."

He spread his hands, palms outward. "I'm just trying to make everyone happy for Christmas."

He wasn't lying about that. If anyone had ever captured the essence of the spirit of Saint Nick, Colonel James T. McGuire had. From the time she was little, even before her mother's death, he'd always tried to figure out what she wanted most and then he'd put all his efforts into getting it for her. Within reason, of course. But since he'd married Gianna, he'd shifted his focus to his wife.

"I thought Gianna already had her Christmas wish. Lucy is due to deliver little Merry any day now."

"She's trying to hold off until after the charity ball."

That didn't surprise Cat. If Lucy managed to pull it off, her stepmother would have all her family around her at the ball and still have her first granddaughter by Christmas.

Her father laid his hand over hers. "Lucia Merceri will only be in town until New Year's Day. And as soon as little Merry arrives, her attention will be diverted."

She managed not to grit her teeth. "And how is Lucia Merceri going to react when she discovers the whole thing was a trick?" Cat jabbed a finger in his direction. "I wouldn't want to be in your shoes when she figures out we lied to her." She frowned. "Matter of fact, I wouldn't want to be in *my* shoes."

"Not to worry." Her father picked up a fork and dug into his stew. "We've got that all worked out. Gianna will just weave her mother another story. A month from now, you're going to have a falling-out with Navy Captain Dino Angelis."

Cat had scooped up a bite of her stew, but the fork slipped from her fingers and clattered back into the bowl. "A month? You can't expect me to carry on this masquerade for a month. I won't."

Her father wiggled his fork at her. "Relax. You'll get through the month just the way you got through the last month—the secret dating and engagement part."

Cat's hands fisted on the table. "The secret dating and engagement part?"

Her father took a manila envelope out of his pocket and pushed it toward her. "The back story is all in there— exactly what Gianna told her mother—from the first time you met to your romantic trysts at the Waldorf right up to when he popped the question on the skating rink at Rockefeller Center."

Cat's eyes narrowed. Her father knew her weaknesses. She loved to skate, but she barely had time for it anymore. "He doesn't skate."

Her father beamed a triumphant smile at her. "He was captain of his hockey team in high school."

She wanted to bang her head on the table. He was outmaneuvering her at every turn. "And just where did you dig up this navy captain who skates?"

"Captain Angelis works for your godfather, Admiral Maxwell. I've already filled the captain in on his back story."

"And he agreed to go along with this charade?"

"Your godfather persuaded him."

Bribed him, Cat thought. Though she'd experienced first-hand just how persuasive Uncle Bobby could be. He was almost as gifted as her father was at making people dance to his tune. She could feel herself weakening.

"Captain Angelis has a two-week leave which he intends to spend with you meeting your family. But who knows? Something might come up, and Bobby could call him back early. The important thing is that we get through the Christmas season and send Lucia Merceri happily back to Rome."

Cat liked Gianna, and she could fully understand the desire to placate Lucia. The woman was scary. She reached for her wine, took another sip, and gave up. "Okay. I'll do it."

"Atta girl. I knew you'd come through for your old dad." Her father dug into his stew. "Eat up. You're wasting away."

Cat ate a carrot, then said, "When do I get to meet Navy Captain Dino Angelis?"

"Tomorrow morning. He's scheduled to arrive at The Cheshire Cat no later than eleven hundred hours."

Cat shifted her attention from her stew to her father. "The store is going to be packed with customers. Shouldn't we meet privately first?"

"When?"

Cat sighed. He was right of course.

"Besides," he continued, "you'll have plenty of time to talk. I've arranged for him to stay in the apartment next to yours."

"He's staying in my building? What about the Waldorf? Isn't that where you said we had our little romantic trysts?"

Her father's brows shot up. "That was when you were keeping your relationship a secret. There's no need for that anymore. Now your job is to convince everyone that your relationship is real. He'll be able to walk you home at night. To all outward appearances, he'll be staying with you." He cleared his throat. "Which is what I assume would be happening if he were your real fiancé."

He reached over and patted her hand. "Besides, with your busy schedule, you wouldn't have any time to go uptown anyway. You couldn't even meet me for drinks at the Algonquin."

Cat mulled it over in her mind.

"The two of you are going to have to spend time together. Lucia Merceri is a sharp woman. She'll be grilling you separately on how you met, when you first fell in love."

Cat stifled an inward sigh.

"Spending time together will give you time to get your stories straight. Make sure you're on the same page. And think of the upside."

Cat's tone was dry. "If there's an upside to this, don't keep me in the dark."

Her father grinned at her. "You'll have an extra person to help out in your store just when you need it the most."

For the second time in as many minutes, Cat badly wanted to bang her head on the table. But she didn't. Her father was right, of course. She could use some help in the store. But he wasn't going to have it all his way. "This navy captain can move in for eleven days. That will get us to New Year's Day. Then Uncle Bobby is calling him back to the Pentagon."

"Deal."

James McGuire held out his hand, and Cat shook it.

4

_____

FROM HIS POSITION in the short alleyway that ran along the side of the Cheshire Cat, Dino had a clear view of the window in Patty's Pub that framed Cat McGuire and her father. When he saw father and daughter shake hands, he knew that his fate had been sealed. He dug his hands deeper into the pockets of his bomber jacket. The sky was clear and the temperature was hovering at the freezing mark. But watching Colonel McGuire persuade his daughter into accepting a fake fiancé had proved highly entertaining.

Dino had arrived while Cat still had customers in her shop—so he could familiarize himself with the area, he'd told himself. Along with his detailed cover story, McGuire had provided a hand-drawn map, so Dino knew that the alleyway emptied into a courtyard that backed into Cat's apartment building and that Cat used it to get to and from work. Not the safest route, he mused.

McGuire's conversation with Cat had not gone smoothly. His daughter had a temper. He'd read it in her body language and in her gestures. There was a lot of raw, pent-up passion in Ms. Cat McGuire, and he knew that was part of the reason he was drawn to her.

Keeping Cat safe was a trickier assignment than any he'd ever taken on under Maxwell's command. It would have been a far easier task if he were just going to be her bodyguard. But the other role McGuire had required—acting the part of Cat's head-over-heels-in-love fiancé and lover—was going to challenge his ability to remain coolly objective.

Even through a plate glass window and at a distance of some fifty yards, he felt the steady beat of desire in his blood. For the first time in his life he wondered if he would be able to control it. He wanted her with an intensity that he couldn't fathom. Nothing, no one had ever pushed him to the edge like this.

Oh, he might tell himself that he had a job to do, and mixing business with pleasure would distract him and possibly jeopardize Cat's life. But no amount of lecturing could erase the vision that he'd had earlier of the two of them making love. Was it a premonition of the future or simply a fantasy? He'd always believed that the Fates offered choices, but he was beginning to wonder if he was going to be able to make the right one where Cat McGuire was concerned.

The other problem—as if his intense attraction to Cat wasn't enough—was he had a strong feeling that James McGuire hadn't told him everything. And going into an operation without all the intelligence that was available was dangerous.

That was why he'd contacted his navy buddy Jase Campbell right after he'd spoken with his mother. Dino not only needed some backup, he also needed Jase's high-tech expertise.

The question was what was McGuire hiding? The most obvious answer was that Cat McGuire was up to her neck in a highly profitable smuggling operation. James McGuire might not believe she was involved—but his opinion was biased.

Dino had to make sure that his wasn't. Cat McGuire might not be aware of the fact that the profits were being funneled to terrorists, but she was the obvious prime suspect to be on the receiving end of the smuggled drugs.

Otherwise, how could it all be happening under her nose? Unless she was stupid, and Dino didn't think she was. Neither did the feds.

At least McGuire hadn't lied about that. There was at least one other person watching Cat and her father tonight. Dino had spotted the man huddled in the doorway of the shop next to the Cheshire Cat when he'd strolled down the street and into the alley. The guy had been too well dressed to be homeless, and he hadn't even bothered with some kind of disguise. Of course, the feds had never been known for their creativity. He himself had brought along a camera, a guide book, plus a shopping bag stuffed with gifts.

When a tall figure moved in the shadows at the mouth of the alley, Dino closed a hand around the gun in his pocket and slipped behind one of the Dumpsters that flanked the alleyway door to Cat's toy store. It wasn't the fed he'd spotted earlier. That guy had been shorter, stockier. He listened, not breathing, for any sound at all. An engine grumbled as a truck rolled past on the street.

The voice when it came was low-pitched and uncomfortably close. "I come in peace. Don't shoot me."

Dino drew his hand out of his pocket. Jase Campbell could move more quietly than anyone he knew. "That was a risky move. I might have shot you."

"Nah." There was a wealth of humor in Jase's hushed voice. "I would have taken you down before you ever drew your weapon. Remember that time in Afghanistan?"

"Yeah." Dino never forgot the times he'd almost bought it. "You saved my life."

"It was a mutual saving that time. Your hunches and my moves. They're a pretty unbeatable combination."

"I hope so." Dino moved out from behind the Dumpster to

where he could once more see Cat and her father. They were eating, and the tension he'd seen earlier had eased. "I need more than your pretty moves this time around. I need your high-tech expertise. Any possibilities on who's leaking information on an ongoing CIA investigation to Colonel James McGuire?"

Jake's chuckle was low-pitched as he materialized out of the darkness. "No proof. But I have a prime suspect. You know, there's a nice little pub across the street. We could have a beer while I report."

"My job and her father are sitting in the window right beneath the Guinness sign."

Jase turned to look and gave a soft whistle. "She's certainly a looker. I wouldn't mind playacting the part of her fiancé."

"You want to bodyguard someone who can't know you're bodyguarding her?" And touch her and kiss her in public and still retain a clear head?

Jase sighed. "There's always a catch to these dream jobs."

"That's where you come in. I need a second set of eyes." He'd filled Jase in earlier on everything he knew about the case—which was limited to what McGuire had told him. Jase was going to provide backup twenty-four-seven. "There's a fed in the doorway next to her shop."

"Not anymore. He took off when I asked him for a match."

Dino grinned. "He'll be back."

"Hopefully, he'll find a more, shall we say, subtle hiding place."

"Where's your man stationed?"

"He's already in her apartment building. I figured you and I could see she got inside safely. You think the danger is imminent?"

"I don't think anything yet. I'm not even willing to believe she's as innocent as her father says she is. I'm just playing it safe. Drugs, money and terrorists. There could be some pretty ruthless people involved in this."

Cat and her father had risen from their table and were pulling on coats as they threaded their way to the door of the pub.

"So who's your prime suspect at the CIA?"

"You're going to love this. Jack Phillips, Cat's uncle and McGuire's brother-in-law by his first wife, is a career man at the CIA. He's never risen up through the ranks because he has a reputation of being a bit of a rogue. He and McGuire aren't on the best of terms, but I figure Phillips might be feeding information to McGuire to ensure his niece's safety."

When Cat and McGuire appeared at the mouth of the alleyway, Dino and Jase faded back behind the Dumpster.

"You know, little girl, you should never take this shortcut alone at night," McGuire said as they passed.

"Daddy, this is a safe neighborhood. Everyone uses this alleyway."

As the voices dwindled, Jase said, "You're going to have your work cut out for you."

In more ways than one, Dino thought. "Let's go have that beer."

CAT LET HERSELF INTO her apartment and flipped the switch that turned on the Tiffany-style lamp in her living room. The switch also turned on twinkling lights on the small Christmas tree on the narrow table behind her sofa.

Dropping her tote on the coffee table, she avoided the sofa. If she sat down, she might be tempted to close her eyes—and then it would be all over for tonight. Exhaustion had slammed into her the instant her father had seen her inside the building and turned to walk back across the courtyard.

She reached the window in time to see him stride out of

the alleyway into the street. A rush of love overtook her. Would there come a day when he couldn't talk her into whatever he wanted her to do?

A fake engagement was the last thing she needed on her plate right now. She had a delayed shipment of dolls, and an assistant buyer who couldn't seem to find a way of contacting her. And twenty-four children might be disappointed for Christmas.

Just thinking about that had a band of pain tightening around her heart. Christmas should be a time of joy, especially for children.

Cat straightened her shoulders. Giving in to worries and anxiety attacks had never been her way. It had never been her mother's way either. She focused her attention back on the courtyard. Magnolia, lilac, and dogwood trees that would bloom beautifully in the spring were now strung with tiny white lights that twinkled like stars.

Christmas was a time for miracles. She'd always believed in that. Those dolls were going to arrive. Tomorrow.

She shifted her focus back to the tall figure of her father still standing in front of the alleyway. She could see the Guinness sign blinking over one of the windows at Patty's Pub. It was going to be tricky catching a taxi at nearly eleven in this section of town. She should have reminded him to call for one when they were having an Irish coffee.

Then a limo pulled up and Orlando, the Merceri family's chauffeur, stepped out. Cat kept forgetting how much her father's life had changed since he'd married Gianna Merceri. But she was so happy for him. She was well aware of how much he'd loved her mother and of how close they'd been. But he loved Gianna, too.

Her lips curved in a smile. Anyone who could find that kind

of love even once was lucky, so she figured James McGuire was doubly so.

Hopefully, one day she'd share in that luck. But right now she had problems to solve: try Matt one more time, check the weather report on the storm that was forecast to slam into Manhattan, and read over the scenario she was supposed to enact starting tomorrow with her never-before-seen fiancé.

For just a second, she rested her head against the window-pane. Well, she'd make it through this. Eleven days wasn't that long. And her father was right—she could use an extra pair of hands in the store.

She might even be able to talk her make-believe fiancé into donning a Santa Claus suit. Cheered by the idea, she was about to turn away from the window and reheat some morning coffee when her eye was drawn to the two men sitting in Patty's Pub beneath the blinking Guinness sign.

Suddenly her senses went on full alert. No. *Full alert* was way too tame a description for the entire-body meltdown she was experiencing. That man—not the one with longish blond hair in a thick black sweater—but the one with hair the color of coal in the black bomber jacket. She'd seen him before.

Racing into her bedroom, she snatched her binoculars off the top shelf of her closet and dashed back to the window. Yes. Yes, it was *him*. She'd only had that brief glimpse of him, but she remembered that slash of cheekbone and that impression she'd had of warriorlike strength. He was definitely the same man she'd seen standing at the edge of the small crowd of customers she'd let into her shop that morning. The same man who'd liquefied her knees and sent her thoughts flying away.

Just looking at him through the binoculars had her heart skipping a beat and her throat going dry. And then the same fantasy that had been teasing at the edges of her mind all day suddenly flooded it. The two of them naked, their bodies locked together and rolling across the floor. A baffling need arose in her to get closer to him—to just go over to Patty's Pub and…what? Jump him?

No. For a moment, she lowered the binoculars and closed her eyes. Then she made herself take deep breaths. She had to get a grip. This kind of reaction wasn't like her at all. She was a rational, sane woman. So she was going to figure out a way to handle it.

Raising the glasses, she looked through them again. First, she was going to take a more objective look. He was leaning against the back of the booth, seemingly relaxed, yet she sensed a kind of leashed intensity in him.

The man with the lighter coloring was more animated. As Cat watched, he threw back his head and laughed. Friends, she thought. And both strangers to the neighborhood.

Her gaze returned to Mr. Tall, Dark, and Intense as he lifted a glass of Guinness and took a long swallow. She focused in on his hands—the wide palms, the long fingers— and her thoughts drifted to what they might feel like on her skin. Every nerve in her body began to throb, her heart skipped another beat, and the same irrational need arose in her to go to him. She'd never had this strong an attraction to a man before.

"Who are you?" she murmured.

As if he'd heard her speak, he turned and looked straight at her. Cat felt the impact of his gaze right down to her toes. And she froze. He knew she was looking at him through binoculars, for heaven's sake. She thought of that moment in Hitchcock's *Rear Window* when Raymond Burr had caught Jimmy Stewart doing the same thing.

A hot wave of embarrassment shot through her, freeing her

from her momentary paralysis. She jumped away from the window and jerked the shade shut. Then she dropped the binoculars on the sofa, and because her knees still felt a little weak, she sat down.

What in the world was happening to her? For the last few minutes she'd been ogling a man as if she were some hormone-driven teenager. More than that, she couldn't seem to rid her mind of the fantasy of having sex with him. Wild, wonderful sex. With a little groan of disgust, she rested her head against the back of the sofa. She had to be working too hard.

When she felt her eyes drifting shut, Cat immediately straightened up. She still had things to do. Snagging the remote, she turned the TV on to a local news station and frowned all the way through the weather report. Not only was the smiling blonde tracking a Nor'easter heading up the coast, but she was also pointing to another storm gathering force over Chicago and pushing through Michigan. Both were due to hit Manhattan sometime tomorrow morning. The banner headline beneath the weather map read The Perfect Storm in red block letters.

But the dolls could already be on their way. Matt had said *tomorrow.* He could have meant the delivery date and not the shipping date. Maybe he'd meant Thursday at the latest. *Please.*

The weather banner was replaced by *Attorney General Jessica Atwell testifying in front of Congress about New York State's new Keep Our Kids Off Drugs program.* For a moment, Cat studied the older woman. She was on television all the time lately due to the success of her antidrug campaign. Adelaide had volunteered in Jessica Atwell's campaign headquarters until the governor had tapped her for the A.G. job. Now with all the publicity Atwell was garnering, there was speculation that she was going to make a run for the Senate. Cat sincerely hoped that Adelaide wouldn't decide to go back and work for her old boss.

Yawning, she turned off the TV. That was a problem for another day. She had plenty on her plate right now. Cat pulled the manila envelope her father had given her out of her tote. After the weather report, maybe the background information on her temporary fiancé would look good by comparison.

On the top of the sheaf of papers she pulled out was a photo of Captain Dino Angelis.

Once again, Cat's heart skipped a beat and her throat went dry. It was *him*—the same man who'd stood outside her shop that morning, the one who was right now having a beer in Patty's Pub. The very same man who'd been toying around at the edges of her mind all day.

And she'd been fantasizing about toying with him. A lot. And tomorrow, he was going to walk into her store and play the part of her fiancé?

No. Cat shook her head firmly. No way. No how. Her life was complicated enough already.

Rising, she rounded the coffee table and paced to the door. She had half a mind to grab her jacket and go over to Patty's Pub and confront him. What had he been doing in the neighborhood this morning and again tonight?

Checking her out?

Whirling, she grabbed the binoculars, strode back to the window, and threw up the shade. The table beneath the Guinness sign was empty. Cat wasn't quite sure whether it was relief or disappointment she was feeling.

Turning, she flung herself down on the couch, then reined in her temper and made herself take several deep, calming breaths. All she had to do was think it through. For starters, she'd given her father her word that she'd play her part in the fake engagement. And she'd always been a woman of her word.

The fact that she was incredibly attracted to the man she was playacting with was just a little bump in the road. In business, she handled those on a daily basis.

And if Navy Captain Dino Angelis *had* been checking her out on the off chance that his role as her fake fiancé was going to have some side benefits? Cat allowed herself one grim smile. Well, she'd just lay out the ground rules for him the moment they met.

In the meantime, Cat pulled the rest of the papers out of the envelope. She'd learn as much as she could about Captain Angelis.

Problem solved.

DINO WAS LEAVING a tip for the maid when his cell phone rang.

"Did I wake you?" Colonel McGuire asked.

"I'm about to leave the hotel."

"You're not due to arrive at the store until 11:00—two hours from now."

Dino didn't tell McGuire that ever since he'd awakened, he'd been feeling a sense of urgency about getting to the Cheshire Cat. Instead, he said, "I have an errand to run."

"An errand?"

"It occurred to me when I was studying my assigned part last night that a crucial prop is missing from the little play you've cast me in." And he'd taken care of it shortly after he left McGuire's office the day before. It was the one detail that the colonel had overlooked.

The brief silence on the other end of the line had Dino biting back a smile.

"A prop?" McGuire asked.

"If we want everyone to believe that Cat and I are engaged, she should have a ring. I didn't give her one when I proposed at Rockefeller Center because we decided to keep the engagement a secret for a time."

Two more beats of silence, and then McGuire cleared his throat. "Good thinking. Of course, she needs a ring. It's the first thing my mother-in-law will notice. Bobby may be right about you."

Let's hope so, Dino thought. Because in spite of everything that McGuire had outlined, the whole charade could go up in smoke, depending on how the scene played out when he walked into the Cheshire Cat.

She'd seen him twice now, so he wasn't quite sure how he was going to play it. Not that he was overly worried. Improvising on the spot had saved his neck many times.

Shouldering his suit bag and his duffel, Dino stepped out into the hall and strode toward the elevators. "Is there something special you called about?"

"Yes. Yes, there is. When I met with Cat last night for drinks, she was worried about a shipment of dolls from that town in Mexico. Paxco. It's been delayed. Could be something's gone wrong on the other end. And if the drugs are in that shipment, she could be in more imminent danger than I thought."

"Then the sooner I get over there, the better."

"Yes. Ri—"

Dino disconnected the call, speed-dialed Jase, and filled him in on the delayed shipment.

"You want me to send someone down to Paxco?" Jase asked.

"No—we don't want to tip off anyone down there. It might panic whoever is on this end. Where is Cat right now?"

"In the Cheshire Cat. She went in at 8:00 a.m. She let in a

woman who fits the description of her assistant manager ten minutes ago."

Dino glanced at his watch. "I'm due there at 11:00, but I'm going to arrive early."

"Got one of your feelings?"

"Yeah." And it was growing stronger with each passing moment.

WHEN THE BELL over the door of her shop jingled, Cat whirled around, nearly dropping the stuffed dragon she'd pulled down from the shelf.

It wasn't him. And it wasn't disappointment she was feeling.

"Easy does it," Adelaide murmured, taking the dragon from Cat to ring up the sale. "The FedEx man never gets here until almost noon."

Earlier, Cat had filled Adelaide in on Matt's garbled message and her hope that the dolls might arrive that day.

"In this weather, all deliveries will be slowed down, so I'd relax if I were you."

Relax? That was a laugh. It wasn't the possible arrival of the delayed dolls that had her heart racing every time someone stepped into the store. Navy Captain Dino Angelis wasn't due until eleven o'clock, an hour and a half from now, and her nerves were already stretched to the breaking point.

In spite of her resolve, she'd dreamed of him, awakened thinking of him. Even after a cold shower and two cups of coffee, she hadn't been able to completely rid her mind of him. Or the fantasies that had filled her dreams during the night. Bottom line, she'd never wanted a man the way she wanted Dino Angelis. How could he affect her this way when they hadn't even met? Hadn't touched? What would it be like when he did lay a hand on her? A shiver of anticipation moved through her. He'd have to touch her, and she'd have to touch him back if they were going to carry off this masquerade. Just the thought had her blood heating, her heart pounding.

Get a grip. Cat glanced around the store which had been teeming with customers ever since she'd opened the doors. Josie was standing behind a table in the far corner offering gift wrap services, and Adelaide was ringing up purchases, leaving Cat free to help customers find that special last-minute gift.

Outside, a good six inches of snow had accumulated on the sidewalks, and as if in celebration, a string rendition of "White Christmas" was flowing out of the speakers. Through it, she caught snatches of conversations. The hot topic seemed to be the storm.

"Looks like everybody had the same idea…"

"…finish my list and get home."

"…catching the 11:00 train out of the city. Otherwise I'll be stuck here."

"The way the weatherman was talking…"

"…expecting to shut down the airports."

When her cell phone rang, Cat dug it out of her pocket and hurried to the spiral staircase to take the call.

"Cat?"

Relief streamed through her at the sound of Matt's voice. "Where are you?"

"I've been stuck in Chicago since 2:00 a.m. The damn storm closed down the airport, but I'm due to fly out in a few minutes. That should get me in before the brunt of the Nor'easter hits Manhattan. According to the weather channels, it's going to be bad."

Cat glanced out the windows. "It's already snowing heavily here. What about the dolls?"

"They aren't there yet?"

"No."

"They will be. I've been tracking the package on my Palm Pilot and they arrived safely at JFK this morning."

Relief was so strong that Cat sat down on one of the steps. "You're sure?"

"Grab a pencil and I'll give you the tracking number."

She dug into her pocket for her notebook. "Go ahead."

When she'd jotted it down, Matt continued, "I wanted to be there when they arrived. They've really brought your mother's design to life, and the workmanship is exquisite. But do me a favor and don't open the box until I get there. There's something I have to explain. Will you promise to wait?"

Cat frowned. "I—"

"Gotta go. They're starting to board my plane. Barring any more delays, I should be at the store shortly before noon."

Matt disconnected and Cat frowned at the phone. She didn't think she could wait for Matt. Once those dolls arrived, she was going to open the package and start calling customers.

The sudden jingle of the bell over the door had her jumping to her feet.

It wasn't *him*.

Instead, it was Mrs. Lassiter. As the grim-faced woman walked toward her, Cat sent her a warm smile. It wasn't returned.

"Are they here?"

"Not in the store, but they touched down at JFK early this morning and I have the tracking number. Our FedEx man usually doesn't get here until around noon." She glanced out the window. "Weather permitting."

Mrs. Lassiter's frown faded, and Cat could almost see relief pouring through her.

"Could I have the tracking number?"

"Absolutely." Pulling her notebook out, Cat read the number off.

She'd just seen Mrs. Lassiter out the door when she remembered she'd promised to call the Santa Claus man. Digging her notebook out, she located the card he'd given her, then hurried behind the counter to dial it.

The call was answered on the second ring.

"Yes?"

Due to the noise in the store, Cat wasn't sure she recognized the voice. "This is Cat McGuire from the Cheshire Cat, and I'm calling a Mr. George Miller."

"Have the dolls arrived?" The tone was clipped and brusque.

"Not yet. But they've landed at JFK, and I have a tracking number for you." Cat read it off.

The phone went dead without a thank-you. Frowning down at it, Cat decided to revise her opinion of Mr. Miller. He was a bit rude to remind her of Santa Claus. But he definitely did remind her of someone.

"Problem?" Adelaide asked.

"I just passed the tracking number for the dolls on to Mr. Miller—that man who cut to the front of your line yesterday, and he's still rude. You're sure you never saw him in the store before?"

Adelaide laughed. "Someone like that—I think I'd remember."

"Well, the computer says he paid for a doll." Cat shrugged. "Matt probably took the order. I'm going to go up to my office for a few minutes. Maybe some of our other customers would like to know that the dolls are at least in the city."

She was on the first step of the stairs when the bell over the door jangled again. Even before she turned around, she could feel him. Turning, she watched Navy Captain Dino Angelis walk into her store.

Beneath the leather bomber jacket, she caught a glimpse of a uniform. A suit bag and a duffel were slung over one shoulder and he carried two grocery bags in his arms.

Here he is. That was the one errant thought that tumbled into her mind before it went blank. A sound filled her head— a rush of white noise that blocked out conversations and the current Christmas carol pouring out of the speaker.

He'd already negotiated half the distance to her, and Cat badly wanted to run. But not away. She felt a pressure in her chest and a strong tug in her belly. If she could have moved, she was very much afraid that she would have run into Dino Angelis' arms.

When he reached her, he dropped everything he was carrying. Now that he was close enough to touch, she fisted her hands at her sides so that she wouldn't lift them to his face. But she wanted to. She'd always thought of herself as a sensible, clearheaded woman. What she was feeling was neither of those things.

This close, the lean face seemed even stronger, and she noted the faint scar beneath his left cheekbone. A warrior's scar.

But it was his eyes that fascinated her. They were the darkest shade of gray she'd ever seen. She thought of black smoke from a fire—the kind that disoriented you, tricking you to move toward the flames instead of away. And there was that intensity in the way he looked at her. She'd been aware of it when he'd stood in front of her shop and again when he'd glanced up from the window of Patty's Pub. It was as if he could read what she was thinking. How could that be?

"I missed you."

Cat wasn't sure whether he'd said the words aloud or she'd

read his lips. Or perhaps she'd spoken them. But how could she miss a man she'd never met?

His hands closed over her upper arms, and then he touched his mouth to hers. It was just the briefest meeting of lips, but his scent surrounded her. He smelled faintly of the sea. And then she caught the first hint of his taste—dark, delicious—and an aching hunger filled her.

Later, much later, she'd wonder what she'd been thinking. She was standing in the middle of her shop, surrounded by customers. But she couldn't think, not when every pulse point on her body had begun to throb, not when greed was building so quickly. So she wrapped her arms around him and pressed her mouth fully to his.

The second taste of him was even better than the first—raw and hot and wonderful. She heard his moan, felt his hands tighten on her arms, and she experienced a whirl of pleasure so sharp that she had to cling to him for support. Suddenly, inexplicably, there was nothing but him. She wanted nothing but him.

IT WAS THE JINGLE of the bell over the door that finally brought Dino to his senses. Even then, he had to call upon all of his willpower to gently unwrap Cat's arms and set her away from him. Baffled, he stared down at her and something akin to fear shot up his spine.

Kissing her had been one of several scenarios he'd considered, thinking that it might be the best way to get over that first awkward moment and at the same time to convince the people she worked with that their "secret" engagement was real. But once he walked into the store and saw her, the kiss had become a certainty. As he'd moved toward her, he'd felt as if his will had been snatched away from him. He'd simply had to taste her.

In the twenty-four hours since he'd first seen Cat McGuire, he'd wondered what it might be like. But nothing had prepared him for the explosion of passion he'd tasted in that avid mouth and felt in that strong, lean body. Nor had he anticipated the strength of his own response—the sharp rush of desire and the burning ache that had driven him to the edge of his control.

He'd never wanted any woman the way he wanted Cat McGuire. He let his gaze drift over the clouded gold-green eyes, the tumbled hair, the lips still swollen and wet from their kiss. Hell. He wanted her right now. No woman had ever exerted this kind of power over him.

But he had a choice. Didn't he?

The bell jingled again over the door of the shop, and he saw awareness creep into her eyes. He sensed in the same instant that the only sound in the store was the bluesy sax playing "I'll Be Home for Christmas."

Gathering his thoughts, Dino wrapped an arm around Cat's shoulders and drew her close to his side as he turned to face a sea of curious faces. He flashed them a smile.

"I wish I could apologize, but I'm Cat's fiancé, and I've missed her."

5

"I THINK THAT WENT WELL." Taking out the key McGuire had given him, Dino unlocked the door of the apartment next to Cat's and led the way inside.

Cat followed him into the room, closed the door and leaned back against it. The space was an exact copy of hers with a small kitchen to the left, bedroom and bath to the right, and a small living room in the center.

He crossed to the sofa in a stride and a half. Setting his duffel, suit bag, and grocery bags on the floor, he slipped out of his bomber jacket and then stepped to the window that overlooked the courtyard. Outside, the heavily falling snow totally obscured the view. But the view Cat was looking at was inside the apartment. Even from the back, the man was beautifully built. The uniform fit like a glove over broad shoulders, narrow waist and hips. When she found herself staring at his butt, she shook her head to clear it. They had important business to settle.

"You think it went *well?*" She purposely hadn't talked to him on the walk across the courtyard or up the three flights of stairs to the apartment. And her silence wasn't due to the howling wind or the blowing snow. She'd learned a long time ago to give her temper time to cool before speaking. But in all fairness, it wasn't Dino Angelis she was angry at. It was herself.

For those few moments when he'd kissed her, she'd lost track of everything but him.

He glanced over his shoulder at her. "I believe Adelaide and Josie have bought fully into our secret engagement story."

"That's why you kissed me?"

"It seemed a quick and effective way to convince them."

How could he stand there talking about it so coolly when she'd been entirely swept away by that kiss? She'd lost track of where she was—who she was. While his mouth had been pressed to hers, devouring hers, all she'd known was a need that threatened to consume her.

Every rational thought had drained out of her mind—and what had poured in was *him.* His taste, his touch, the feel of that rock-hard body pressed against hers. She'd never experienced anything like it. Even now, looking at the lean length of him, desire flared again—hot, urgent, necessary.

Get a grip, Cat! There had to be a way to handle this. She narrowed her gaze on him as he shifted his attention to the brown bags.

"I stopped in the little grocery store on the corner and picked up provisions. They're predicting that this storm will shut down Manhattan before the afternoon is over. I got plenty for both of us—if you want to borrow."

He glanced around, then carried the bags through the archway into the small galley-shaped kitchen.

She watched while he unloaded food and wine, storing some of it in the refrigerator and tucking the rest away in cupboards. It looked like a lot of stuff to her and it drove home the point that he was here to stay. Until New Year's Day, she reminded herself.

His movements were slow, precise. How could he appear to be so cool and collected while she felt hot and wired? It had been the same way in the shop. Temper bubbled up as she recalled the easy way he'd introduced himself to Josie and Adelaide while she'd stood there focusing all her attention on getting some feeling back in her knees.

Within minutes, Dino Angelis had charmed the two older women into accepting the romantic story of their secret engagement. Two of her regular customers had congratulated her, and Adelaide had insisted that Cat take Dino to her apartment and get him settled in. She and Josie could manage for a while on their own.

After folding the bags and storing them, Dino turned, leaning a shoulder against a cupboard. "Convincing Josie and Adelaide was only part of the reason why I kissed you."

He was looking at her in that intent way again, and it made her toes curl. It suddenly occurred to her that they were standing as far apart as they could get in the small room. And he'd been the one who'd created the extra distance by moving into the kitchen. Perhaps he wasn't as cool as he wanted her to believe.

"What was the other part?"

"I also kissed you because I wanted to. I'd been thinking about doing it ever since I first laid eyes on you outside your shop yesterday morning."

Me, too, Cat thought. And she'd fantasized about doing a lot more than kissing. Right now, she was thinking about walking to him, unbuttoning that shirt and getting him out of it. Reaching behind her, she closed one hand around the doorknob to anchor herself. "Don't do it…again."

A smile curved his lips, and Cat saw a dimple flash on his right cheek.

"Now that we know what it's like, we're both going to want to do it again."

She already did. What was wrong with her? Pressing her palms flat against the door behind her, she straightened her shoulders and pushed herself away. "We're adults."

"Agreed."

"Reasonable, intelligent adults. We don't have to act on our impulses."

"No argument there."

But…

Though neither of them spoke the word aloud, it hung in the air between them. And Cat knew that if one of them moved toward the other right now, being reasonable or intelligent or even an adult wasn't going to matter.

Temper surged through her again. "I don't want to feel like this."

"The Fates don't always offer what we're looking for."

She frowned at him. "The Fates?"

His eyes were steady on hers. "I was raised in a Greek family. We believe strongly in the Fates and the choices they offer us. Sometimes they surprise us."

Dino Angelis was a surprise, all right, and Cat wasn't at all sure that she had a choice where he was concerned.

That scared her. She was used to having some control over herself. Her life. She ran her hands through her hair and began to pace. "Look, I don't have time for this. I don't even have time to think about this right now. I should never have agreed to this charade of my father's."

"Are you thinking of backing out?"

Her chin lifted as she turned to meet his eyes. "No. I agreed to do this fake engagement thing, and I keep my word."

For the first time she wondered if he was any happier about the situation than she was. She'd read in the background information her father had provided that he had family in San

Francisco—family he wouldn't be joining for Christmas. "Are *you* thinking of backing out?"

"No. I keep my word, too."

Cat studied him for a moment. "It's got to be hard for you. Don't you want to spend the holidays with your family?"

"Yes."

"Then why did you agree to do this?"

Dino met her eyes. "Sometimes, I can just feel things and know that they're right. When your father asked me to take this job, I knew that I was meant to do it."

"So you're saying it was fated? Inevitable?"

"I suppose."

Fate. Inevitability. Hadn't she felt a similar way when she'd first opened the Cheshire Cat? And when he'd walked into the store earlier, hadn't her first thought been—*Here he is?* No, she couldn't allow herself to think that way.

"I didn't expect…" She raised her hands and dropped them. "…everything to be so…complicated."

"Complicated is one word for it." He straightened from the cupboard. "If it will help, now that we've established the credibility of the engagement, I can promise that I won't grab you and kiss you again. When we kiss the next time, it will be a mutual decision."

There was something in his tone and in the way he looked at her that made her believe him. Some of her tension eased.

"I'm going to stow my things, and we'll get back to the Cheshire Cat."

She led the way down a short hallway to the right. "The bedrooms and bath are this way. This apartment has the same floor plan as mine." When they reached the bedroom, she stood aside and let him enter.

He unpacked his suit bag and hung a dress uniform on the

clothes tree in the corner of the room. Then he dropped his duffel on the foot of the bed and unzipped it. "Before we go back to the store, I have something for you."

Cat recognized the trademark blue of the designer jeweler the moment he pulled the small box out of his bag, and her heart took a little tumble. He opened it and held it in his outstretched hand as he walked to her.

Her throat was dry as she stared down at the ring. A marquise-cut emerald caught and reflected light in an oval ring of diamonds. He lifted her hand and slipped the ring onto her finger.

Something touched her then—more than the warmth of his hand, the firmness of his grip. She felt a sense of rightness. Of inevitability?

A bubble of panic rose. This was a make-believe engagement with a man her father had maneuvered into taking her on as a job. James McGuire had no doubt provided the ring as window dressing—along with the background story he'd given them both. Still, she said, "It's lovely."

"It fits?"

She nodded. For the life of her she couldn't seem to take her eyes off of the ring. Nor could she find the strength to pull her hand out of his.

"I chose the emerald because of your eyes, but I had to guess at the size."

She met his eyes then. "You bought this ring?"

He nodded. "I believe it was the only detail that your father missed. But I figured it might be a telling one. From what your father has said of Lucia Merceri, a missing engagement ring would catch her attention."

Wincing, Cat nodded her head. "She'd pounce on it like a hungry dog on a bone, and she wouldn't let go until she had an explanation."

"The more I hear about this woman, the more curious I am to meet her."

Cat nearly smiled as she met his eyes. "Be careful what you wish for."

Dino glanced back down at their joined hands. "The ring looks good on you. In my experience, it's often the small things that make an operation go south."

An operation. The two words brought Cat out of her little trance and stiffened her spine. Oh, the ring was a telling detail all right. It was a symbol of their fake engagement—designed to fool everyone. She'd do well to remember that.

Pulling her hand out of Dino's, she said, "I need to get back to the store."

"Of course." Placing a hand on the small of her back, he guided her out of the room and down the short hallway. "When we get back there, put me to work. For the length of our engagement, I'm at your service."

DINO SAT BACK on his heels and blew out a long frustrated breath. Cat McGuire had taken him at his word and assigned him a challenging task. The moment they'd gotten back to the store, she'd escorted him up the circular iron staircase to a large room on the second floor that she used as an office. Then she'd asked him to put together a dollhouse that she'd promised a customer before closing that day. He'd noted that the dollhouse had been shipped from Paxco, Mexico.

As far as he could see, the package hadn't been tampered with, and there'd been nothing in it but the promised dollhouse, which was as tricky to assemble as a thousand-piece jigsaw puzzle. He was halfway through when she appeared at the top of the stairs. "Is it finished?"

"Just the first floor."

She dropped to her knees, selected one of the wall pieces that surrounded him and snicked it easily into place.

"I can see you're an expert," Dino said.

"Practice makes perfect. I've done quite a few of these. My first one took me over three hours."

Dino picked up a second piece of wall. When it didn't immediately slide into place, her hand covered his.

"Sometimes, you have to finesse it like—" She broke off when his fingers closed around hers. The piece of dollhouse clattered to the floor.

Dino hadn't been conscious of taking her hand. It had just seemed to happen. Her fingers were slender but strong, and they returned the pressure of his.

They touched nowhere else, but they were close, their knees nearly brushing, their bodies leaning toward each other. In that moment, he recalled exactly what her body had felt like when it had been pressed to his—the melting softness, the heat. God, he wanted to touch her. He wanted to slip that sweater over her head and let his hands slowly, very, very slowly mold every inch of her. He wanted to feel the silky texture of that bare skin beneath his fingers.

When his gaze dropped to her mouth, he remembered exactly how she'd tasted, the initial tartness, then the incredible depth of the sweetness. Hunger built fiercely inside of him. Her lips were parted, moist and so close that he could feel her breath mingle with his. He shifted his gaze to her eyes. They were wide and clouded with the same desire that he was feeling.

If either of them moved…

He could have her, Dino thought. They could have each other. Right now. Right here. In seconds, he could make the vision that had been tempting him, tormenting him ever since he'd first seen her, a reality.

But that wasn't what he'd promised her. He'd told her he wouldn't grab her and kiss her again. Summoning up all his control, Dino released her hand, picked up the piece of wall and slipped it into place. "I can take it from here."

"I—yes." She scrambled to her feet. "Right. I'll get back to work."

She was as rattled as he was. He took some satisfaction in that as he watched her descend the stairs. He wanted her way too much for comfort, and he was beginning to think way too much for his own sanity. How many more times was he going to be able to draw back before he took what he wanted?

CAT DIDN'T KNOW how she made it to the bottom of the stairs. Layers of mist still clouded her brain, and her legs felt as if they'd dissolved below the knees. The Cheshire Cat was filled with customers, laughing, talking, but all she could hear was the loud hammering of her pulse. She wondered why everyone in the store didn't turn and stare at her.

Gripping the stair railing, she drew in a deep breath and willed her brain cells to click back on again. They'd begun to go into meltdown the instant Dino's fingers had gripped hers.

For heaven's sake, all he'd done was take her hand in his. There'd been no other point of contact between them, and yet it was as if he'd touched her everywhere. She'd imagined exactly what it would be like to have those hands on her bare skin, her shoulders, her throat, her breasts. She'd felt the hardness, the urgency, the ruthlessness. An almost unbearable thrill had moved through her.

And when he'd nearly kissed her again… Lord, she'd wanted him to. More than that, she'd willed him to. Even though she knew that if his mouth had taken hers, neither one of them would have stopped with a kiss. They would have made love right there on the floor of her office without any care at all for the fact that just below, her shop was filled with customers.

Gathering her scattered thoughts, Cat focused her gaze on her store, her customers. But even as she stepped off the stairs and managed a smile for one of them, she wondered how much longer she would be able to resist what she was feeling for Dino Angelis.

BY FOUR O'CLOCK THAT AFTERNOON, Dino was ready for a break. He felt as if he'd been on a particularly demanding set of maneuvers. After finishing the dollhouse, he'd taken the time to search her office. She kept the space militarily neat. The desk was large, free of clutter, and the paperwork in the two filing cabinets all related to her toy business. There was a small refrigerator stocked with bottled water and a carved oak cabinet that contained a bottle of good brandy and four glasses.

Over her desk, there were a series of sketches, each one of a different doll, and they were all signed by Nancy McGuire, Cat's mother.

At noon, Cat had asked him to run across the street to the pub and bring back sandwiches—which the three women had somehow managed to grab bites of between customers. Though he hadn't liked leaving Cat in the store, the errand had allowed him to spot the location of the federal agent. He was across the street today, but he was still standing out like a sore thumb. Dino hadn't been able to spot Jase's man, which had reassured him.

His most recent assignment had been to clean up her back storeroom. As far as he could tell the small space was used mostly for stashing deliveries until the toys could be unpacked and put out on display. From the buildup of clutter, he surmised that it might have been a week or more since anyone had had time to put the room in order. Small wonder if the Cheshire Cat had been as busy in the past two weeks as it had been today.

Opened boxes had been piled everywhere. None of them had been shipped from Mexico. Adelaide and Josie had dashed in frequently to grab an armload of dragons or pirate ships to replenish the ones that were flying off the shelves. Cat had so far stayed away. That was making it easier for him to keep his mind on his real job.

While cleaning, he'd taken time to check out her security system. While it was a good one, he figured that someone with Jasc's expertise would be able to bypass it without much trouble.

There were two entrances. The one at the front of the store and the one in the storeroom that led out to the alley that ended in the courtyard of her apartment building. If he were going to break in, he'd use the alleyway entrance.

So far, there'd been no sign of the delayed shipment of dolls. Gut instinct told him they were the key. They had to be. And the longer the dolls were delayed, the more danger Cat might be in.

Taking one last look out into the shop to assure himself that Cat was safely involved with a customer, Dino propped open the side entrance to the store, grabbed an armful of collapsed boxes and made his way to the Dumpster.

Cat entered the storeroom just in time to watch Dino exit. When she caught herself staring at his backside, she shook her head in disgust. Since she'd fled down the stairs from her office, they'd mostly managed to avoid each other. But that hadn't kept him out of her mind. And in spite of how busy she was, she'd caught herself more than once looking for him. At him. Each time she did, memories and sensations came flooding back and she wanted him more. Her body wasn't paying one bit of heed to any resolutions she might have made.

Shaking her head to clear it, she tried to remember what she'd come into the storeroom for. First baffled, then annoyed, she scanned the shelves for a clue that would trigger her memory. And there it was. The toy soldier. *That's what you came for—a* toy *soldier, not a real one.*

It was on the very top shelf, of course. Grabbing the ladder, she edged it along the floor to a spot directly below the toy, and then scooted to the top rung. But it was just out of reach. Rising to her toes, she stretched her arm to its full length and closed two fingers around the rifle.

Beneath her, the ladder swayed and teetered. Getting a firmer grip on the soldier, she fought for balance. She was losing the battle and praying that she wouldn't break something when the ladder suddenly steadied and two large hands closed firmly around her calves.

"Steady now?" he asked.

"I'm fine."

Still he took her arm and guided her to the floor. Cat could feel the pressure of each one of his fingers just below her elbow. They burned her skin like a brand. A longing filled her to feel his hands move over every inch of her. And to have her hands on him. His throat was at her eye level, and she could see the rapid beat of his pulse. Her own raced to match its rhythm.

Thoughts drained away and a noise filled her mind—the sound of the wind before a storm. She should step back. Dimly, she was aware of a pressure building inside of her. Hunger was too tame a word. This was greed. Irrational. Compelling.

Once again, it was Dino who broke the contact, dropping his hand and backing away. "You should be more careful."

"Yes." She couldn't have agreed more. Her reaction to the man might confound her, but one thing was becoming crystal-clear. Whenever she came near him, she wanted him. It was that simple. That primitive. That inevitable?

"Thanks for the help."

"No problem."

Oh, yes it was. But it wasn't fear that moved through her as she walked into the front room of the shop. It was a wild thrill.

FIGHTING AGAINST THE URGE to go after her and drag her back into the storeroom, Dino waited five beats before he moved to the doorway. She was handing the toy soldier to an excited customer.

What in hell was he going to do about what he was feeling for Cat McGuire? If this were an op, he'd have a strategy in place by now. His mind and his body would be working in harmony. But with Cat, what his mind was telling him to do was at total odds with what he wanted to do.

She was…well, she was something he'd never experienced before. He'd known from the moment he'd first seen that photo of her that something might happen between them. But he'd never anticipated the power of their attraction, nor the way it was escalating. On both their parts.

Each time he touched her, his control was being stretched to the breaking point. Soon, Dino knew that he wouldn't be able to back away. And the worst way to address the problem was to stand here staring at her like some totally bewitched adolescent.

Turning back into the storeroom, Dino tried to find something else to do. But the room was already neat. He'd stacked boxes against one wall and placed the toys he'd unpacked on the shelves that lined two walls. In the process he'd unearthed a small refrigerator stocked with soft drinks and bottled water. Next to it was a narrow table and two chairs. On the shelf

above the fridge was a teakettle and one of those fancy cof-
feemakers that produced one cup at a time. His mother had a
similar one in her office so that she could always offer her
clients fresh brewed coffee.

On a slow day, Dino could picture Cat racing in to grab a
drink or a quick cup of coffee. What he couldn't picture her
doing was sitting down at that table. The thought had him
frowning slightly. The woman worked tirelessly, and she never
seemed to walk when she could run. Then, because he could
no longer help himself, he moved back to the doorway and
glanced out into the shop. Just as he'd suspected. Even now
she wasn't still. She was leaning against the counter scribbling
in the small notebook she carried in the pocket of her skirt.
There was only one harried-looking shopper left in the store.

Customers had thinned steadily since noon. Outside, the
falling snow was so thick that it blocked the lights of the pub
across the street. Cars and trucks on the street progressed at
a snail's pace. But they were still moving. Cat had sent Josie
home at one and insisted that Adelaide leave shortly after that
so that she could take the subway uptown before the rush hour
backed everything up.

Both women had protested vehemently.

"You'll need help when those dolls arrive," Adelaide
had argued.

"Dino can help me," Cat had countered as she'd handed
Adelaide her coat.

"What about the phone calls? You promised to call
everyone as soon as the dolls were here."

"I can do those. Now go."

Josie had been an easier sell, but she'd reminded Cat that
she could be back at a moment's notice if she was needed.

Dino had to wonder if Adelaide's and Josie's reluctance to

leave had anything to do with the fact that the dolls hadn't been delivered yet and they wanted to be in the store when the FedEx man finally arrived. Each seemed to sincerely care about the shop and the customers. And he'd observed enough of Cat's relationship with Josie and Adelaide to know that she trusted them both implicitly. Either one of them might be the "inside man" who identified the toy carrying the drugs and made sure it got to the person behind the operation.

His gaze returned once more to Cat. As if she felt it, she glanced up, and in the moment that their eyes met and held, Dino once more became aware that the clock was ticking. He was simply not going to be able to keep a handle on what he was feeling for her much longer.

AS SHE LOOKED INTO HIS EYES, Cat felt a pull as strong and inexorable as the pull of the moon on the oceans. Her skin was tingling, her pulse pounding. And all he was doing was watching her. What would happen when he touched her? Really touched her? Her time for deciding what to do about Dino Angelis was running out. If they'd been alone in the store, she might have gone to him right then and done what she'd been fantasizing about doing all day.

She dragged her eyes away from Dino's to check on her lone customer. The woman, a stranger, was currently in a relaxed browsing stage. A shopper at heart, Cat decided to give her new customer five more minutes before offering to help.

She resisted the urge to look at Dino again. She knew he was still in the doorway to the storeroom because she could feel the heat of his gaze on her skin.

Think of something else. The dolls.

The man was even distracting her from what had been the topic most on her mind before she'd met him. In spite of the earlier crush of last-minute shoppers, she'd managed to keep track of her package from Paxco. And it was on its way. As soon as the dolls arrived and she'd notified the people who'd bought them, she and Dino Angelis would be going back to her apartment building. Once inside, they *could* go their separate ways. The curtain would descend on their little act until the next day. It was the simple solution.

So why did she suddenly want complicated?

Cat nibbled on the end of her pencil and frowned. In other situations in her life, business, family, she could always figure something out. She even knew how to handle her father.

Glancing back down at her notes, Cat reviewed the list she'd made. Writing things down always helped her to think more clearly. #1—*I'm* extremely *attracted to Dino.* Cat drew a second line under the word *extremely*.

#2—*I really, really want to have sex with Dino Angelis.* Hot, uncomplicated, outrageous sex. He'd shown her so much with one kiss. Was she going to be able to live without knowing more about what he could do to her?

Or about what she could do to him?

#3—*If I pass on this opportunity, will I ever have another chance?* She thought of what Dino had said about the Fates offering surprises. Well, Dino Angelis might be the biggest surprise she'd had in her life so far. He'd already stirred things in her that she'd never felt before.

It was a fake engagement. In Dino's words, an operation. It couldn't go anywhere—so what if they decided to simply enjoy each other? What on earth could be wrong with that? They were both adults. She tapped her pencil on the page of the notebook. Reasonable and intelligent adults.

Her lips curved when she realized she was using the same

argument she'd used with Dino earlier—only this time for a different outcome.

Her gaze dropped to the ring she wore on her finger, and something tightened around her heart. The problem was that the ring didn't feel fake. She fisted her hand. In fact it felt just right.

#4—*I like him.* Until yesterday morning he'd been a complete stranger to her. And though she still didn't know much more about him than her father had detailed in the file, she felt she was coming to know him. For starters, he was a hard worker. And he hadn't objected once during the day as she'd ordered him around.

Cat tapped the eraser of her pencil against her bottom lip. He hadn't complained when she'd shown him the dollhouse. And there was something about his presence that inspired... what? Confidence? Now that she'd gotten a little distance and some perspective, she had to admit that his entrance into the shop and the way that he'd kissed her had been a stroke of genius. Adelaide and Josie had bought into the secret engagement one hundred percent. And they were completely charmed by him.

Cat frowned down at her notes. Why did she suspect that liking him was going to complicate things?

Stop overthinking it.

Dragging her eyes away from her notes, Cat glanced around her store. Hadn't she spent the last several years of her life focusing on her career and achieving her dream of owning her own toy store? Maybe her father was right for once, and she ought to take some time to smell the roses. Or to just simply enjoy Dino Angelis.

She let her gaze drift to the door of the storeroom. Dino had his back to her, as if making one last check on the cleanup he'd done. From the front the man was a knockout, but his backside came in at a close second. She felt that pull again, strong, sure, and an aching need moved through her. Of all the toys in her store, Dino Angelis was the one she wanted most from Santa.

"Miss?"

Reining in her wandering thoughts, Cat focused on the worried-looking woman standing in front of her.

"I just can't decide. My son David is seven. He's a reader, does well in school. He doesn't go in much for sports. Do you have any suggestions?"

"Do you think he might like a magic set?" Cat led the way to the front of the shop where she'd displayed a selection of beginning magician kits. "I sell a lot of these to young boys who are smart and have a serious turn of mind."

DINO WATCHED Cat escort her last customer to the door. The woman's harried expression had been replaced by one of delight.

"I can't thank you enough, Ms. McGuire. It's the perfect gift for my David."

"Most days I have the best job in the world," Cat said as she opened the front door. "I hope that you and your family have a lovely Christmas."

In the brightly colored green sweater and print skirt, Cat reminded Dino a bit of a butterfly. They were elusive, hard to capture, but definitely worth the chase. He desperately wanted his hands on her. He recalled the way she'd felt in his arms—slim, supple and strong. He wasn't sure what he was going to do when they finally returned to the apartment building. Go their separate ways? That would be the smart move. But he wasn't sure he'd be able to make it.

The rush of cold air from the open door did nothing to diffuse the heat that arrowed through him as a seductive fantasy blossomed in his mind. The lights were low, and there was music playing—something muted on a saxophone. She was standing only a few feet away. Slowly, she pulled the sweater up over her body, revealing that pale, delicate skin one inch at a time.

What she wore beneath it, the froth of white lace and silk that barely covered her breasts, had his breath backing up. Her flesh was smooth and delicate as alabaster. For a moment he simply let his eyes absorb her while the need to touch her grew into a burning ache. He could vividly imagine the contrast between the slight roughness of the finely crafted lace and the petallike softness of her skin.

In his mind, he reached out to trace a finger over the swell of flesh above her bra when Cat suddenly vanished through the door of the shop.

Dino blinked, refocused. But his eyes hadn't deceived him.

One second she was there and the next, all he could see was a swirl of blinding snow. Panic streaming through him, Dino raced for the door. "Cat!"

6

WHEN DINO CRASHED into her, the impact unbalanced both of them. Gripping her shoulders, he staggered back against one of the display windows, pulling her with him.

Cat struggled to break free. "He's here."

"Who's here?" Dino shifted in front of her as he peered through the blinding snowfall.

Cat wiggled out from behind him, pointing into the street. "Ted. The FedEx man."

Dino made out the shape of a truck that was double-parked in front of the Cheshire Cat. Swiping snow off of his eyelashes, he finally saw the darker shape of a man moving toward them. Once more he pushed Cat behind him.

"Cat McGuire?" a gravelly voice asked.

"Who wants to know?" Dino asked.

"That's me." Cat spoke at the same time and this time she didn't wiggle. She gave Dino a good hard shove and stepped around him.

The man was close enough that Dino recognized a delivery man's uniform, but they were easily come by. He was carrying a large box, poised on his shoulder in much the same way a skilled waiter would balance a tray.

Even as Dino inserted himself between Cat and the delivery man, Cat said, "You're not Ted."

With one hand Dino gripped Cat's arm firmly. He slipped his other one into the pocket of his jacket and closed his fingers around his gun.

"No, ma'am. Ted ran into some trouble. Could you sign here?"

"Do you have some ID?" Dino asked.

"ID? Look, buddy. Go check my truck. There's an 800 number. In the meantime, I've got a delivery from Mexico." He set the box on the ground and passed an electronic signature pad to Cat.

The wealth of tiredness in the man's tone did more to convince Dino than anything else that he was looking at a true FedEx delivery man. "What kind of trouble did Ted run into?"

As Cat scrawled her signature, the man elaborated. "He got held up. Can you imagine that? You live here in this city, and eventually you see everything. He'd just gotten a signature when two thugs in a van pulled up alongside of him, pointed a gun at him, and told him to open the back of his truck."

"They robbed him?" Cat asked.

"Nah. Luckily, some concerned citizens witnessed the attempted robbery and dialed 911. Not that there would have been a quick response in this weather. But one of our mounted policemen happened by, and between the angered witnesses and the horse and the fact that the policeman was armed, the two men jumped in their van and took off. This city gets a bad rap a lot of the time, but those people were pissed. I mean there were probably Christmas presents in there."

"There were," Cat said as she handed him her signature.

"Ted was pretty shook up, as you might imagine, and since I was nearby when he called the incident in, I offered to deliver some of his packages."

"You're a true Good Samaritan," Cat said. "This box contains a Merry Christmas for twenty-four children."

"Happy holidays," the man said as he disappeared into the thickly falling snow.

Dino shouldered the box. "Let's get this inside." Carrying it half propped on his shoulder the same way the delivery man had, he urged Cat back into the store.

"I'm assuming you want to unpack these now," he said.

"Definitely. I've been so worried about them that I won't be satisfied until I know they're all here. Then I promised to call each person who ordered one of the dolls and give them the good news."

Her eyes shifted to the shop window. All she could see was a blur of snow. "The worst of this is supposed to be over by midnight."

"Why don't you lock up the store and set the alarm while I carry these upstairs? Your office offers the most space, and you wouldn't want anyone just wandering in while we're working."

No, she didn't. Cat studied Dino as he strolled to the spiral staircase and climbed them. She opened her mouth, and then shut it. What he'd said about locking up was smart. She was sure she would have thought of it. Eventually. Once she'd assured herself that the dolls were all here. But something in the way he'd said it had set her nerves a bit on edge.

Turning, she flipped the Open sign to Closed, then locked the door and turned the alarm on. Hurrying to the storeroom, she checked the locks on the door that opened onto the alley and made sure the security system was activated there also.

No, it wasn't that he'd reminded her to lock up that had her nerves jumping. It was the way he'd grabbed her out in the street and shoved her behind him—almost as if he'd believed she was in some kind of danger.

Which was totally ridiculous. She swept her gaze around the Cheshire Cat as she strode to the spiral staircase. What safer place could there be than a toy store? The fact that some Scroogelike thugs had tried to rob a FedEx truck four days before Christmas was just one of those crazy things that happened in Manhattan.

As for Dino's overly protective attitude, she could probably lay the blame for that on his military background. Her father often displayed the same annoying traits.

Her nerves a bit more settled, she ran up the stairs and discovered that Dino had already opened the box and was holding up one of the dolls. Moving toward him, she held out her hands. "Matt was right. They are more beautiful in person."

He gestured to a framed sketch over her desk. "It's the same doll, isn't it? Did you design it?"

"No, my mom did."

"You must be so proud."

"I am." Something in her throat tightened as she took the doll. It had a face of delicately painted porcelain. The brunette hair was pulled back and then fell in curls almost to her waist. The silk dress was a rich shade of red. "It's been my dream to bring one of her sketches to life. But it wasn't until I discovered these wonderful craftsmen in Paxco, Mexico, that I was able to accomplish it. Next year, we'll add a second design and people can begin to collect."

"Take a closer look," Dino advised.

Turning the doll over, Cat saw that an inch of lace had pulled away from the hem of the dress, and the pantaloons beneath the dress were soiled. Frowning, she thought fast. "I can fix it. Let's check the rest."

It wasn't until they'd unpacked all of the dolls and matched them to the order slips she'd retrieved from the file in her tote bag that Cat relaxed.

"I count twenty-five," Dino said.

"And twenty-four are in pristine condition. Thank heavens I ordered one for myself at the last minute. I can take the one with the torn lace and repair it. I'm going to surprise my father with it. He's so hard to buy for."

She picked up the damaged doll and examined it. "Maybe this one delayed the shipment. Matt may be able to explain it when he gets here."

"Matt?" Dino asked.

"Matt Winslow is my assistant buyer. I sent him down to Paxco the day before yesterday, the moment I learned about the delay. He got stranded at O'Hare overnight, but when I talked to him last, he was boarding a plane for JFK. He was supposed to get here at noon. Things have been so hectic that I completely forgot."

"Any planes coming into JFK or LaGuardia were probably delayed," Dino said. "Did Matt know you'd ordered the extra doll?"

"I never mentioned it to him. I told him to ship whatever dolls were ready." She recalled her earlier conversation with him. "He asked me to wait for him before I unpacked the dolls. He seemed concerned about something. Perhaps because this one was damaged." As she spoke, she carefully stored it in her purse.

DINO RESTED HIS HIP against her desk and willed himself to ignore the stab of jealousy her words and the expression on her face had caused. For the first time, he wondered what kind of a relationship she had with Matt Winslow. Certainly not a serious one if she'd agreed to the pretend engagement with him.

She stepped toward him and set her tote on the desk. They were standing so close that he could reach out and touch her.

Keep your mind on the job. He carefully tucked his fingers in his pockets. "What's he like?"

She met his eyes as she considered. "Matt is very business-focused. He's smart, good-looking, and he thinks in creative ways."

How creative, Dino wondered. Creative enough to put the drugs in the damaged doll? Dino very carefully avoided looking at her tote bag. He let himself consider reasons why the dolls hadn't shipped on time. Perhaps the drugs had been delayed on the Mexico end and the last-minute rush had caused one of the dolls to be treated carelessly. The soiled pantaloons and torn lace would make it easy for someone on this end to identify it. Is that why Winslow had wanted to be present when the shipment was opened? The condition would delay the sale of the doll—perhaps until the customer it was meant for walked into the store.

"I'm lucky to have Matt," Cat continued as she settled her hip on the desk. She nearly brushed against him as she did.

Dino tucked his hands deeper into his pockets.

"But working for me is just his stepping-stone to something bigger."

"Bigger like what?"

She laughed, and as the bright bubble of sound filled the room, Dino realized two things. He'd never heard her laugh before. And he wanted to hear the sound again—and often.

"Matt wants to be a millionaire someday. He's not going to accomplish that here at the Cheshire Cat."

For a moment as he looked at her, Dino felt every thought drain out of his head. Maybe it was the way she was smiling at him. Or perhaps it was her eyes. Lit with laughter, they reminded him of that shade of green that was so peculiar to the color of the sea around the Greek Isles. Whatever it was, he felt abruptly and completely enchanted. Unable to stop himself, he reached out and touched just the ends of her hair, rubbing a curl between his fingers. In spite of the fiery color, it felt cool against his skin.

She'd stopped talking and he recognized the growing sensual awareness in her gaze. When she moistened her lips, he nearly broke his promise not to grab her and kiss her again.

"I've been thinking," she said.

"About what?"

She lowered her eyes to his mouth, then raising her hand, she brushed one finger along his bottom lip.

"I've been thinking about kissing you again. But first…"

Abruptly, she dropped her hand and strode to the center of the office.

Dino came very close to breaking his word. His lip burned where she'd touched him. How hot would they both burn when he kissed her again?

She whirled back to face him. "I want to do more than kiss you. I want to have sex with you."

WHEN HE TOOK A STEP toward her, she wanted badly to just shut up and run into his arms. But she held up both hands. "First, let me finish." She drew in a deep breath. "I've thought it all through. I even listed the main points in my notebook."

His brows shot up. "That's what you were writing about?"

She nodded. "I want you to know up front that I understand the ground rules."

"Ground rules?"

Cat waved a hand, nearly losing her train of thought when light sparkled off her engagement ring. "That this is just an operation to you. To me, too. At my father's request, orders really, we're pretending we're engaged until the holidays are over. It's kind of like being Cinderella at the ball. Poof. Everything goes back to normal at the stroke of midnight on New Year's Eve. You'll go back to working for my godfather at the Pentagon, and I'll go on with my life here. I can live with that. But…"

"But…?" He waited in that quiet, intense way he had, and her thoughts threatened to spin away.

Ruthlessly, she gathered them. "But no one has ever made me feel the way you do." She took a tentative step toward him. "I want to know what else you can make me feel. I want to know what I can make you feel."

The heat in his eyes gave her the courage to continue. "You talked about the Fates offering choices. I suppose that the safer option would be to try to keep our distance."

Anxiety had her turning to pace. "Normally, I choose the safer path. I'm not much of a risk-taker." She whirled to face him. "But I don't want to keep my distance. I don't see any reason why we can't enjoy each other. Maybe the Fates are offering us an opportunity to give each other a Christmas present."

"A Christmas present?"

Her heart was beating so fast Cat wondered if he could hear it. She drew in a deep breath and let it out. "I was thinking earlier that of all the toys in my store, you're the one I most want to play with."

"You're sure?"

Nerves danced in her stomach, but as each second ticked by, she became even more certain. "Yes."

He moved toward her then in that slow gait that ate up the ground. *Thank God,* was all she could think. But he stopped when she was still out of arms' reach.

Suddenly, her temper surged. "Do you feel the same way about this or not?"

"Oh, we're on the same page."

"Then why don't you grab me and kiss me. You have my permission."

"First, take off your sweater. While you've been jotting down pros and cons in your notebook, I've been fantasizing about seeing you naked."

Suddenly both her temper and her tension eased. She shot him a smile that widened when she saw the gleam of amusement in his eyes. Slowly, she unbuckled her belt and dropped it to the floor. "The difference between the male and the female mind?"

He nodded. "We're simple creatures at heart."

Maybe that was true for most men, but Cat didn't believe that of Dino Angelis. Not for a moment. There were layers to him that fascinated her every bit as much as the physical attraction.

Cat slipped her hands beneath the edge of her sweater and drew it slowly up and over her head. The slight scratchiness of the wool rubbing over her skin was erotic, but when he dropped his gaze slowly from her throat to her waist, she felt singed.

"I was imagining white lace, but the pale green is very nice."

"Thanks. Now it's your turn." She moved to him and began to unbutton the shirt of his uniform. "I've been thinking about doing this all day." When the last button had been freed, she slipped her fingers beneath the shirt, running her hands over his skin as she shoved it down his arms. The garment had a tailored fit, and as she'd watched him lift and carry during the day, she'd gotten a good idea of the planes and angles of his upper body. Still, looking at his bare skin, her palms went damp.

"Problem?" he asked.

"Yes," she managed. "You still have too many clothes on."

"It's your turn again."

She hadn't thought it was possible to get any hotter without turning into a puff of steam. But she'd never stripped for a man before—never helped a man to strip for her.

Getting into it, Cat ran her fingertips from her throat, over her breasts to the waist of her skirt. Then she unhooked it, wiggled her hips and let it slide to the floor.

The quick catch of his breath sent a fresh thrill of pleasure through her. She knew what he was looking at. She had a weakness for expensive lace underwear, and she favored thigh-high stockings. She'd chosen the sea-foam green in honor of the Christmas season. The high boots were for fashion, as well as protection against the inclement weather.

For ten humming seconds, Cat didn't think Dino was going to be able to unglue his gaze from her legs. When he finally met her eyes, she thought she just might melt into a puddle of lust.

"I thought I was going to be able to prolong this." He moved then, closing the distance between them. When he gripped her waist, and lifted her, she felt like a featherweight. "Hold on."

She wrapped arms and legs around him, her head spinning as he strode to the wall and pressed her against it. His mouth covered hers for one drugging kiss. She sank into it. If she were offered a choice between survival and this, she'd choose this.

No man had ever had this power over her. No one had ever made her feel this helpless. But it wasn't fear that streamed through her, it was delight as he ran his hands over her in one possessive sweep, pressing here, molding there. He slipped fingers beneath her thong and she nearly came when he penetrated her heat.

She quivered, moaned his name, then cried out in shocked protest when he lifted his mouth from hers. Desperate, she arched helplessly, trying to get closer to him as he rained kisses over her face, her neck, and closed his teeth around one nipple through the lace of her bra.

"I can't seem to get enough, can't seem to get a grip on control where you're concerned."

His words were a hot breath at her ear.

"No problem." She tried desperately to pull his mouth back to hers. "Kiss me again."

He pressed her more firmly against the wall, and she felt the hard strength of his desire pushing into her center. Helpless, she pumped against him. But she couldn't get close enough, not with the fabric of his trousers separating them.

"I need some help." His voice was ragged.

Together they jerked at his belt, yanking the snap of his pants open and dragging down the zipper. As he struggled to shove the fabric down his hips, she wrapped her hand around the hard length of him, guiding him toward her.

"The condom."

"What?"

"In my back pocket."

Condom. Cat tried to wrap her brain around the concept as she reached around him and pulled it out. Together, they fumbled to sheath him.

"Now. For heaven's sake, now!"

She wasn't sure if she'd shouted the words or just thought them. Finally, just when she wasn't sure if she could survive another second, he drove into her. His thrusts were fast, hard. Glorying in it, she moved with him.

"Again. Again. *More*."

This time she was almost sure he'd said the words, over and over until they became a chant in her head, a beat in her blood.

He battered her against the wall, they battered each other until the orgasm ripped through her. She was still shattering into small pieces when she heard his cry of release.

7

WHEN HE COULD FINALLY THINK again, Dino had no idea how Cat had ended up sitting on his lap on the floor, her head snuggled against his neck. Her hand rested against his bare chest, and the emerald caught and reflected the lights from the Christmas tree.

It was just a symbol of their temporary arrangement, he told himself. That was why it looked so right on her finger—because it was right for now. Just as making love with her was right for now.

No regrets, Dino promised himself. He'd chosen to take what the Fates, what Cat had offered. And he wouldn't lie to himself. Making love with her once wasn't going to be enough.

"I think that went well," Cat said.

Realizing that she'd repeated the exact words he'd used after he'd kissed her that first time, Dino threw back his head and laughed. When she joined him, he pulled her close in a friendly hug.

"Touché. And it did go well." He drew back from her then and met her eyes. "But I'm thinking there may be room for some improvement." He traced a finger down the side of her neck. "We could give it a shot."

Downstairs, someone pounded on the door.

"Ignore it," Dino murmured against her mouth.

Cat pressed both of her hands against his chest. "I can't. Technically, the store should still be open."

The pounding grew louder.

"And I left all the lights on."

With a sigh, Dino eased her off his lap, and they both reached for clothes. Dino finished dressing first and hurried down the stairs. He could make out two figures huddled in front of the door.

"It's the Santa Claus man and Mrs. Lassiter. I know they're both anxious to get their dolls, but how in the world did they make it back here in this storm?" Cat said from behind him as she punched numbers into the alarm pad.

"Santa Claus man?" Dino asked.

"When he walked into the store yesterday, I thought there was something familiar about him, and I decided it was because he looked a bit like Santa. His real name is George Miller."

"He isn't a regular customer then?"

"No."

"What about the woman?"

"Mrs. Lassiter is in here all the time. And she's evidently desperate to get her doll. They both must be to come out in this storm."

Dino opened the door, and a tall woman and a portly man entered the store.

"I came to pick up my doll." The man spoke directly to Cat. "You're supposed to be open until seven."

"I closed early because of the weather. How did you know the dolls had arrived?" Cat asked.

"You gave me the tracking number," Mrs. Lassiter said.

"Right," Cat said. "And then I called and gave it to you, Mr. Miller. You'll have to forgive me. It's been a long day. I'll get them for you."

As Cat hurried up the stairs, Dino studied Mr. Miller. The white hair and mustache along with the glasses did create a certain resemblance to Santa Claus. What interested Dino even more was that Cat wasn't familiar with him.

"Do the two of you know each other?" Dino asked.

Miller glanced at the woman next to him. "No. Why?"

"You both arrived at the same time."

Mrs. Lassiter flicked Miller a glance. "Coincidence."

"How did you both manage to make it back into the city?"

"I decided to stay at a friend's in the city overnight," Mrs. Lassiter said. "Who knows how long it will be before they clear away all this snow. The doll is very important to my granddaughter."

"And you, Mr. Miller?" Dino asked.

Miller pushed his glasses up on the bridge of his nose and studied Dino. "I live in the neighborhood."

Cat raced down the stairs carrying dolls and two Cheshire Cat gift bags. "Here they are."

She handed a doll to each customer so they could see them before she put them into the gift bags. "Merry Christmas. I hope you don't have far to go in this weather."

"You'll be open tomorrow?" George Miller asked.

"Yes." Cat opened the door for them. "The snow is supposed to stop at midnight. I'm sure that by tomorrow, New York City will be back to business as usual."

Dino thought hard. He didn't like the fact that two of the dolls were leaving the shop before he'd had a chance to search them. He'd been hoping to sneak back into the Cheshire Cat tonight and accomplish that. He hadn't anticipated that two customers would come early.

He studied Cat as she reset the alarm. If she had handed over the drugs just now, how had the doll been matched with the right customer? They were all identical, each a faithful match to the drawing over her desk, and when he and Cat had worked, side by side, unwrapping each doll, she hadn't shown favoritism to any one, hadn't looked for any special markings. She'd simply pulled them out of the box and lined them up in the order in which they'd been unpacked.

Dino shoved his hands into his pockets. Was he actually considering the possibility that she was involved? Perhaps that was a sign that he had at least some objectivity left where she was concerned. But while they'd unpacked the dolls, he *had* looked for markings, and he'd found none.

The only doll that had been different was the one she'd stuffed into her tote. Watching her re-alarm the system, Dino went with his gut instinct. Even if the doll in her tote did contain the cocaine, Cat McGuire wasn't involved. Everything he knew and sensed about her as a person told him that she wouldn't have used her mother's dolls in this kind of an operation.

THE PHONE RANG. A glance at the caller ID brought on a surge of panic. It rang again. Ignoring it wasn't an option.

"Yes?"

"You were supposed to be there when the shipment of dolls arrived."

Lying wasn't a good idea when the voice at the other end of the line was this emotionless. "I couldn't be there. This weather—"

"I don't tolerate excuses."

The flat tone of the statement had fear joining the panic.

There was a beat of silence, then, "The dolls are in the shop right now. I want you to get me mine."

"How?"

"I'm going to give you a number to call. 758-3712. When

the man answers, tell him what you need. Remember, there are consequences for failure."

The line went dead.

Breathe. There's still a way to solve the problem. Just dial the number.

The fingers that punched the numbers into the phone trembled.

INCOMPETENT BUNGLERS. That's what they all were. First down in Paxco and now at the toy store. For nearly a year, the operation had run without a hitch, and suddenly people were dropping the ball right and left.

Fury welled up. It never paid to depend too much on others. As soon as the going got a little rough, they began to panic. And then the mistakes always multiplied. Temper bubbled up again.

Walk off the anger. It will only cloud the issue. It's your cool head that's gotten you this far. Think.

It wasn't too late. There was still time to get the drugs before the danger became too great. But there was no doubt the threat of exposure was growing. Cat McGuire was a smart woman. Perhaps too smart. If she started to put two and two together…

Anger faded abruptly as a plan formed. There was a way to eliminate the problem. The hand that punched numbers into a cell phone was as steady as a rock.

DINO CLOSED CAT'S BEDROOM DOOR and moved quickly through the small apartment to the kitchen. He'd left her in the bathroom drying her hair. The temptation to linger and watch while she did it had been strong. But he'd already given in to too many temptations where she was concerned.

He hadn't been able to prevent himself from joining her in the shower. He'd watched her eyes darken to a deep emerald green when he'd carefully laid the condom in the soap dish. A fresh wave of heat engulfed him as the memory seared through his mind.

"I'm not going to make it out of here without having you again," he'd said.

"Fine with me."

He'd taken the soap from her hands and rubbed it between his own. "But first, I'm going to wash you slowly from head to toe."

And he'd delivered on his promise. At last, he'd had his hands on her skin, something that he hadn't taken much time to do when they'd made love in her office. He'd lathered her neck and her breasts. Then he'd lingered for a while on her bottom before he'd thoroughly explored the slick, silky skin of her legs. Her eyes had misted over and her breath had become ragged before he'd finally slipped two fingers into her and made her come, once, then twice. Then again.

The water had turned cold before he'd put on the condom, lifted her and buried himself in her. He'd struggled to keep his thrusts slow, but she'd dug her nails into him, cried out his name, and he was helpless to do anything but drive them both into the madness.

With a frown, Dino shook his head to clear it of the memory. The woman had completely enchanted him. When he wasn't making love to her, he was thinking about it. And his need for her was already interfering with the job he had to do. He glanced back at the bedroom door. He couldn't be near her and not want her. But his job was to keep her safe, not naked and beneath him.

And that was only part of the problem. Her proposition had been for uncomplicated, "poof, it's over at the stroke of midnight" sex. But when he'd slipped that ring on her finger, something had clicked for him. And each time he made love to her, it clicked again. But that wasn't something he could think about now.

Shaking his head again, Dino wondered if he would ever be able to completely rid his mind of her. Then he pulled his cell phone from his pocket. He could still hear the hum of the hair dryer, but he had no idea how long it would take her to finish. This might be his only window of opportunity to call Jase. Dino punched the numbers in.

"Yes?"

"I don't have much time. Two names—Lillian Lassiter and George Miller. Check them out." During the process of helping Cat call all of her customers who'd ordered dolls, he'd noted the full names on the order slips.

"Are those the two I saw visit the store after you closed?"

Dino's brows shot up. "Right. I thought you had one of your best men assigned to the store tonight."

"One of my best men is stranded in the Bronx, so you're stuck with yours truly. Nothing is moving in this mess."

Dino moved into the living room to assure himself that the hair dryer was still running. A glance out the window told him that the storm was still at full throttle.

"As you no doubt saw, the FedEx man delivered the dolls, but I didn't have a chance to search them for the drugs."

"I can handle that. It will get me out of the cold."

"Be careful. You may not be the only one checking them out."

"Got one of your feelings?"

"Maybe. Watch your back and keep me updated. The next time you call, you'll be my cousin Nik."

"You got it."

The moment, Dino pocketed his cell, he strode back to the kitchen. They'd stopped at his apartment earlier, and he'd picked ιp what he'd need to fix them a meal. He couldn't risk searching the doll in her purse until later when she was sleeping.

CAT LOOKED AT HERSELF in the full-length mirror. How did one dress to have a home-cooked meal with one's lover?

She'd decided against work clothes, but she certainly wasn't going to wear the sweats she wore on the rare occasions when she lounged around the apartment. So jeans and a red silk shirt it was—she refused to change again.

Impatient with the fact that her hair was still damp, she'd pulled it into a ponytail and fastened it with a red scrunchy. Not the most glamorous hairdo, she decided, but it would have to do. Stepping closer to the mirror, she studied her image more closely. When was the last time she'd dressed with a man in mind?

And Dino Angelis was no ordinary man. She grinned at her reflection. In fact, he might be the very best Christmas present she'd ever given herself. Her body was still tingling at several pulse points from how he'd touched her in the shower. She'd known that making love with him would be incredibly exciting, but she hadn't anticipated the half of it. Nothing, absolutely nothing had come close to what she'd done, what she'd discovered with Dino.

She'd never thought of herself as a particularly sensual person, but he had set her inner sex siren free. So much so that she couldn't wait to make love with him again. And why not? The dolls had arrived safely. By tomorrow, they would all be in the hands of their new owners. Wrapping her arms around herself, she twirled once in front of the mirror before she strode to the door.

The moment she stepped into the living room, she stopped short and her heart fluttered up to her throat. The scene Dino had created assaulted her senses. There was music, something low and bluesy, but she couldn't take her eyes off of the red checked tablecloth spread on the floor and the two fat candles burning on the coffee table. The only other lights in the room twinkled from the small Christmas tree.

When he'd said he'd cook a meal for her, she hadn't expected a picnic in December.

The scent coming from her kitchen pulled her like a magnet. But when she reached the archway, it wasn't the food that had her mouth watering. It was the man. He was wearing coal-colored jeans, a black turtleneck sweater, and his feet were bare. Unlike his uniform, these clothes fit him like a second skin and incredibly, her palms began to itch. In her mind, she pictured him without the clothes and her insides went into a meltdown.

Get a grip. She shifted her gaze to his hands as he moved chicken breasts from a skillet into bowls and ladled sauce over them. Although the aroma drew her, all she could think about was how those wide, hard palms had felt on her skin. What those long fingers had felt like as they'd moved inside of her.

He didn't have to kiss her or touch her to make her want him. He just had to *be.*

How in the world can you want to jump him so soon after what you did to each other in the shower?

"Can I help?"

He turned and slowly swept his eyes over her. "You could pour some wine."

If he continued to look at her like that, she was going to drag him to the floor. And if he could tell what she was thinking, he'd suspect she was a nymphomaniac.

With an effort to control herself, Cat moved to the uncorked bottle sitting on the counter and tipped wine into two waiting asses. Turning, she watched him sprinkle some freshly chopped herbs on top of the chicken breasts, then place a knife and fork in each bowl. When he'd finished, she handed him a glass, then took a sip of her own.

Say something. Anything.

"When you said you were going to whip something up, I didn't expect gourmet fare. Did the navy teach you to cook like this?"

"No. All the Angelis men can cook. My cousins and I grew up in our family's restaurant, The Poseidon." Leaning a hip against the counter, he took a drink of his wine. "You'd like it there, I think."

Cat knew from the file her father had given her that Dino had lost his father and aunt in a boating accident when he was eleven and that his mother and uncle had blended the two families.

"My uncle was hoping that one of us would eventually take over the restaurant and continue in the family business, but it didn't happen. However, there's still hope. My cousin Nik has married a caterer, and last year my uncle Spiro married Helena, a five-star chef from Greece. So there's still a good possibility that an Angelis will take over The Poseidon one day. My mother who has strong psychic powers predicts that Angelises will run the restaurant for some time."

"Your mother has psychic powers?"

Dino nodded. "She has a very successful practice in San Francisco."

Cat tilted her head to one side and studied him for a moment. "You said earlier that you accepted the job my father offered because you had a 'feeling' that you should. Do you have psychic powers, too?"

Dino shrugged. "Sometimes I get hunches. It seems to run

in the family. All of my cousins seem to have inherited some kind of power. Philly's is the strongest. She has a special gift with animals."

He handed her his glass, then balancing a loaf of bread on one of the bowls, he lifted them. "This isn't really picnic fare, but there's no place in your apartment to eat."

"You noticed." Cat led the way into the living room.

When they were seated with the steaming bowls in front of them, Dino broke off a piece of bread, dipped it into the sauce in her bowl and offered it to her.

Cat tried it and the flavors exploded on her tongue. Once she'd swallowed, she said, "What did you put in there?"

"Wine, garlic, oregano."

Eager now, she took the piece of bread he offered and dipped again. "It's marvelous."

"Where do you usually eat?"

She sliced into the chicken. "Restaurants mostly. Or I do takeout and eat it in my office or standing up in the kitchen."

She chewed and swallowed, and then sighed. "This is so good. If I thought I might be able to accomplish something like this, I'd take cooking lessons."

"I could teach you."

She grinned at him over the rim of her wineglass. "I'll give you fair warning. I've been known to burn water."

He met her eyes. "I love a challenge."

Trying to ignore the little thrill that moved through her, she set her glass down and cut another piece of chicken. "You know, we're still practically strangers."

"Ask me anything you want."

"You're very close to your family."

He handed her another piece of bread. "As close as brothers and a kid sister can be. We were raised in the same house, learned to sail and fish together. And fight together. Except for Philly. We kept her out of our fights. Mostly."

"I've often wished for a brother or a sister. Not that my father didn't try to fill a multitude of roles after my mother died. When my uncle Jack's around he tries to play big brother."

"What's your uncle like?" Dino asked.

"Hmm." Cat considered while she took a sip of wine. "My Uncle Jack is like Peter Pan—he never quite wants to grow up. And he's pretty good at playing big brother. It's just that you can't talk to your father or your uncle about boys. Or fashion."

She wrinkled her nose. "I learned early on not to take my father shoe shopping. He told me after our first shoe excursion that he understood for the first time why some soldiers went AWOL."

Dino threw back his head and laughed. As the rich sound of it filled the room, Cat felt her heart flutter again. It occurred to her that she felt very much at ease sitting here on the floor of her living room with this man she'd known for less than a day. In fact, she felt more at home than she ever had before.

Oddly disturbed by the thought, she turned her attention back to finding out more about Dino Angelis. "If you were so close to your family, why did you leave San Francisco?"

Finished with his meal, Dino leaned back against the coffee table and reached for his wine. "From the time I was a little boy, I had this feeling that I was meant to join the navy. I suppose it was partly because all the Angelis men are drawn to the sea. My father is descended from Greek fishermen and my mother's father was a ship builder in Sausalito."

Studying him in the flickering candlelight, Cat could easily picture him on the sea—hauling in fishing nets or at the helm.

She could also imagine him as a craftsman, running those capable hands over the helm of a sleekly crafted boat.

She recalled from her father's file that he'd worked special ops, and her first impression of him was that he looked like a warrior. Yet, today in her store, he'd played the role of a helpful fiancé perfectly.

Was being her lover just another part of the op for him? And why should that bother her? After all, she'd outlined the parameters of their relationship, hadn't she?

She stacked their empty bowls and carried them out to the kitchen. After rinsing them, she inserted them neatly in a dishwasher she rarely used. When she turned, she found he'd followed her with their empty wineglasses. He reached around her to place them on the counter, and his body brushed against hers.

The rush of heat was immediate and strong. This close, she caught his scent—her soap and something very male.

She moistened suddenly dry lips. "Playing a fake fiancé has to be a far cry from what you're used to. I'll bet you'll be relieved on New Year's Day when you can get back to working for my godfather at the Pentagon."

"Actually, Admiral Maxwell is expediting my discharge papers."

"You're leaving the navy? Why?"

"You could say I'm following one of my feelings again. I miss my family and I want more balance in my life."

She met his eyes steadily. "Do you always act on your feelings?"

"Almost always." He reached out to tuck a stray curl behind her ear. "Like right now, I want to make love to you again." Leaning down, he angled his head and nipped at her ear. "Have you ever made love in your kitchen?"

"No." But she placed both hands on his chest when he started to draw her closer. "I can't remember ever acting just on my feelings before. I don't understand it."

"Do you have to?"

"I usually like to. I prefer to have a goal so that I know where I'm going. I like to map out all the details. With you it's different. I don't want to think about the future and I don't want to consider the consequences. I just want to live in the present. You're a first for me, Dino."

"You're a first for me, too, Cat."

Hearing him say it and seeing the truth of it in his eyes, she felt a tight band inside of her ease. "I don't know where we're going."

"Neither do I." He took her fingers and raised them to his lips. "We don't have to. All we have to do for tonight is enjoy each other."

She smiled at him then. "I have one request."

His eyebrows rose. "Only one?"

"I want to touch you. All over. But first, I want you out of your clothes." She took his arm, running her hand from his shoulder to his wrist and linked her fingers with his. Then she drew him with her through the archway.

8

"I WANT TO SEE YOU NAKED," Cat said. "That's how I imagined you when I first saw you in the kitchen tonight."

"Really?"

"Oh, yes. And it's not a habit of mine to undress men in my mind." Pausing in front of the coffee table, she turned to study him. "Perhaps it's because I didn't get to see enough of you in the shower. That space is pretty confined."

Raising their linked hands, he pressed his lips to her fingers. "I didn't notice."

She pulled her hand free and slipped it beneath the edge of his sweater. "Let's get you out of this."

Together they pulled it off and dropped it on the floor. Watching the twinkling lights of the tree flicker over the golden tone of his skin, her desire for him sharpened and Cat fisted her hands at her sides. She had a plan. "As a navy man, you're used to following rules?"

"You could say that."

Slowly she shifted her gaze to his. "I only have one for you. You can't touch me until I'm through touching you."

"You're asking for a hands-off policy?"

"Exactly."

It had been a mistake to look into his eyes. The smoky heat she saw there was a mirror image of her own feelings, and for a moment she completely lost her train of thought. All she had to do was step forward, press her mouth to his, and she would once again experience that whirlwind of passion he could sweep her into. Fighting against the temptation, she shifted her attention to his lips and traced the shape of them with one finger.

When he drew it into his mouth and nipped it, an arrow of pleasure shot right to her toes. "The rules…"

"I didn't touch you. Yet."

Cat drew in a shaky breath and dragged her gaze determinedly to his shoulders. She ran her palms over them, absorbing the surprisingly silky texture on the surface and the hint of steel-hard muscles beneath. The contrast fascinated her as did the difference in their skin tones. Finally, she gave in to the temptation to explore his chest, grazing his nipples with her nails and then watching them harden.

Unable to resist, she leaned closer, gripping his waist for balance as she used her tongue and teeth first on one nipple and then the other. Each of his responses—his sharp intake of breath, the hiss of her name, the rapid beat of his heart—thrilled her.

Once again, she wanted to move closer, but remembering her goal, she fought off the urge. Instead, she ran her hands up to his ribs and around to his back.

"You have the sexiest back. I can't tell you how many times I caught myself staring at it today." That was the ticket, she thought. Just keep talking. She ran her nails lightly down his spine to his waist. "As soon as I have you out of the rest of your clothes, I want you to lie down on the sofa and I'll give your back the attention it deserves. But first…" She pulled open the snap of his jeans.

"I'm betting we don't make it to the sofa."

Cat didn't reply because it was taking all her concentration to lower his zipper. Biting down hard on her lower lip, she started to drag down the snug fitting jeans.

"Wait."

Stilling her hands, she glanced up in time to see him dig into his back pocket and drop condoms on the table.

"Three." The sight of them sent such an intense surge of heat through her that Cat was surprised she didn't just liquefy on the spot.

"Since I go with my feelings, I like to be prepared."

Cat sank to her knees and refocused her attention on tugging the jeans down his legs. Beneath them, he wore a pair of black briefs, stretched almost sheer, that clearly revealed the size of his erection. In some part of her mind that was still functioning, she knew that together, they managed to strip the jeans off, but she couldn't tear her gaze away from those briefs and what they were trying to cover.

Swallowing to moisten a dry throat, she said, "It's like a present."

"Consider it yours." Dino wasn't sure how much longer he was going to be able to follow Cat's rules. Then he simply stopped thinking when she traced a finger down the length of him.

"On Christmas Eve, I always snuck downstairs once everyone was asleep and I would touch each one of my presents, lifting each package and shaking them. It was torture knowing that I couldn't open them."

"You're a big girl now, Cat."

"Yes. I am." She drew down the briefs, and Dino stepped out of them.

For a moment, neither of them spoke or moved. Each time she exhaled, he felt the heat of her breath on his penis. And above the mournful sound of the jazz trumpet, Dino was certain he could hear the beat of his own heart. Or was it hers?

"It's going to blow my plan to hell, but I have to touch you." Then she closed a hand over him and milked him in one long pull.

"Cat—" He had to shift one of his feet to keep his balance.

"You like that?"

His only reply was a moan when she pulled her hand along the length of him again.

"Let's try this."

Dino came close to losing his balance again when her mouth closed around him. He couldn't breathe, could barely think. Yet, every one of his senses had sharpened. He was aware of the slow steady wail of the trumpet, of the way the Christmas tree lights brought out the darker red highlights in her hair, of the sharpness of her fingernails as she dug them into his buttocks. But mostly he was aware of how that hot, avid mouth was dragging him closer and closer to the edge of reason. And he was powerless to stop her.

He'd experienced desire before—the wild and reckless kind, the warm and needy kind. But no woman had ever made him weak. Helpless. His arms felt like lead. And when she began to suckle him, taking him deeper and deeper into the wet, hot recesses of her mouth, he felt the orgasm begin to build at the base of his spine.

But he wanted to be inside of her when he came—when they both came. The unbearable need for that intimacy gave him the strength to close his hands around the sides of her head and gently draw her away. He managed to maintain some control until he sank to his knees and they were face to face.

"I'm not through yet," she said.

"I don't always follow the rules." Then he crushed her mouth with his.

The kiss was desperate and demanding, exactly what Cat was craving. She heard the rip of silk, but later couldn't recall any other details of how her clothes had disappeared. All she could remember was those fast clever hands as they raced over her, pressing, possessing. She knew exactly what he was feeling because she was experiencing the same mindless pleasure. No one had ever set her this free with a touch. Reveling in it, she dug her nails into his shoulders to keep him with her when he tried to draw away.

"Condom," he said.

In the twinkling lights of the tree she watched him kneel and sheath himself. Then he made a place for himself between her thighs. Drawing him in, she wrapped arms and legs around him, then met him thrust for thrust. The storm built quickly until it far surpassed the one that had been battering the city all day.

"Look at me."

His face was above hers, filling her vision and her world. And she felt herself sinking into that dark, intense gaze.

Just before she did, she said, "Come with me."

Increasing the speed of his thrusts, he took them both over the edge.

DINO PAUSED in the doorway to Cat's bedroom, studying her sleeping form on the bed. It was the only time she was completely still. Since he had no idea how sound a sleeper she was, he'd waited, not moving, for fifteen minutes after her breathing had become steady.

She'd curled into him in sleep, throwing her arm across his chest as if to keep him there. Lord help him, he'd wanted to stay. Incredibly, he'd wanted to wake her and make love to her again. But the clock was ticking. This might be his only chance to search the doll Cat had tucked into her tote. And it was beginning to bother him that Jase hadn't called him back.

A glance at his watch told him it was nearly midnight, almost three hours since he'd talked to him. Surely, it wouldn't have taken the man this long to search those dolls.

He spotted Cat's tote on the narrow table behind the sofa. Shutting the bedroom door, he crossed to it, careful not to tread on the clothes they'd left scattered on the floor. The snow had stopped, and stars dotted a clear black sky.

Stepping closer to the window, he glanced down at the courtyard. Lights were twinkling on the trees, and a floodlight from the back entrance to the apartment building illuminated much of the area. Only the alleyway was shrouded in darkness. Still, Dino caught a movement near the door to the Cheshire Cat. Grabbing the binoculars he'd noticed earlier, he lifted them and focused the lens.

Two figures were fighting in the opened doorway to Cat's store. They were about the same height, both shorter than Jase, and appeared to be well matched. Locked in a fierce embrace, they tumbled onto the floor of the alley, rolled across it, each one claiming, then losing the upper position.

For an instant, they were out of sight behind a Dumpster. Then one scrambled to his feet and headed in the direction of the courtyard. The attempt at escape was prevented when the other figure took the first one down in a hard tackle.

Dino set down the binoculars and quickly pulled on his jeans and sweater. Where in the hell was Jase?

Damn! He'd left his shoes in Cat's bedroom. Moving quickly to the door, he eased it open, spotted his shoes near the foot of the bed, and retrieved them. He'd covered half the distance to the living room when Cat said, "Where are you going?"

He turned back. "I couldn't sleep. I thought I'd watch one of your movies."

She yawned hugely and threw back the covers. "I'll join you."

Dino thought fast while she pulled a robe out of the closet. "You should get some sleep. You have a busy day tomorrow."

She shot him a smile. "So will you."

By the time she'd closed the distance between them, Dino decided to go with the truth. "Look, I spotted two men fighting in the alleyway by your store. And the door to the Cheshire Cat is open. I'm going to check it out."

"I'll go with you."

"No." He grabbed her by the shoulders. "I'm trained to handle this kind of thing. You're not. You'll just get in my way. And every minute I spend arguing with you, they could get away."

EVEN AS HER HEART RACED, Cat stopped struggling and stared at him. There was something in his tone—the ring of command?—that had her saying, "Okay. Okay."

Feeling a bit numb, she stood in the bedroom doorway and watched as he grabbed his leather bomber jacket, then met her eyes again. His were cold as steel.

Suppressing a shiver, she wrapped her arms around herself. This was a side of Dino Angelis she hadn't seen before.

"Lock this door when I'm gone. Understand?"

She nodded. But as soon as he'd disappeared, it was the window she rushed to. Grabbing the binoculars, she focused on the alley. It was deserted, but the door to her shop was open. How—and then she saw him.

Not two men but one, sitting in the snow at the courtyard

end of the alley way, his back propped against the brick wall of a building. One of his hands was gripping his shoulder, and the twinkling lights on the courtyard trees winked on and off across his features.

The face was familiar. Cat's heart shot to her throat and lodged there. She allowed herself a few more seconds as the lights blinked on and off. The time only made her more certain. The man sitting in the snow was her uncle Jack.

And he was hurt.

Fear iced her veins, as questions spiraled through her mind. How? Why?

Where was the other man and where was Dino?

Dropping the binoculars onto the couch, she grabbed jeans, struggling into them as she half ran, half hopped into her bedroom. She dragged a sweater over her head, shoved her feet into boots and raced out the door.

It had to be a dream. A nightmare. She burst through the door to the stairwell and flew down the three flights. *Uncle Jack.*

What had he been doing in the alleyway? When she finally ran into the courtyard, the only man she saw was Dino. He was crouched down near the spot where she'd seen her uncle. As she reached him, she stumbled.

Strong hands gripped her shoulders and steadied her.

"I told you to stay in the apartment."

"I couldn't." Cat still stared at snow, at the impression where a man had been seated. "Where did he go?"

"Where did who go?"

"The man." She glanced down the alley way, but the snow had been so disturbed that no footprints were visible. "He was sitting right here. I was sure it was—"

She broke off the moment she saw it—the dark red stain right near the wall of the building. A fresh surge of fear moved through her as she tore her gaze away from it and met Dino's eyes. "That's blood, isn't it?"

"Yes. Who do you think you saw?"

"I thought—but I must have been mistaken. It doesn't make any sense. My mind's playing tricks on me." She clamped her lips together as she heard the hysteria rising in her voice.

Dino gave her a shake. "Who do you think it was, Cat?"

"My uncle Jack." Drawing in a deep breath, Cat gathered herself. It wouldn't do to fall apart. She had to think.

"Your uncle Jack Phillips who works for the CIA?"

"Yes. But he called me just a few days ago from Mexico. Surely, he would have told me if he was coming to New York."

"Why did he call?"

"To chat. He wanted to know how sales were going, if I was overworking myself."

"Do you know where in Mexico he called from?"

She shook her head slowly as she narrowed her eyes. "Why are you asking all these questions? And how do you know my Uncle Jack works for the CIA?"

DINO ANSWERED THE LATTER QUESTION and prayed it would distract her from the first one. "Your father mentioned it in your file."

"And you didn't see him when you reached the courtyard?"

"No. There was no one here." Dino glanced down the alleyway, but during the course of their fight, the two men he'd seen had crushed down a lot of the snow. "Did your uncle have the code to your security alarm?"

"No."

"But as a CIA agent, he probably possessed the skills necessary to bypass it."

Cat twisted out of his grip, her eyes narrowing further. "Just what are you suggesting?"

Dino jerked his head in the direction of her shop where the door stood wide-open. "Someone got into the Cheshire Cat tonight, and they didn't set off the alarm."

Before he could stop her, she was past him, running toward the shop.

"Cat." He followed and grabbed her hand, halting her as they reached the door. He couldn't send her back to the apartment because he couldn't be sure that she'd be safe there. Just as he couldn't be sure that Jase was in any condition to provide backup.

"I'm going to have to take you in there with me, but you're going to have to stay behind me and follow orders."

"This is my shop."

Even in the dim light, he could see her eyes glint with anger.

"And right now the man who hurt your uncle may be in there. Judging by the blood stains, I think we can presume he's armed."

Deliberately, Dino removed his gun from his pocket. "I want your word that you'll stay behind me and follow orders."

Her gaze had dropped to the gun and she swallowed hard. "All right. Yes."

Dino felt something twist in his gut. He'd meant to scare her and he had. But he shoved his feelings aside and, flattening himself against the wall, reached round to turn on the light.

The room was empty. Still using his body to shield Cat, he closed the door behind them.

"Reset the alarm."

He led the way across the room, gripping the gun with both hands. Dino's instinct told him that both men he'd spotted fighting in the alley were long gone. But he wasn't about to take any chances.

In the doorway to the front of the shop, Dino once again flipped on the light, then fanned the room with the gun.

"Stay here," he whispered to Cat. Then he moved forward, keeping his back to the wall. Finally when he'd checked every hiding place he waved her to him.

"Can you tell if anything's missing?" he asked softly.

Without saying a word, she moved to the cashbox behind the counter and checked it.

"The money is all here," Cat whispered. "There wasn't much. We do most of our business by credit cards." Then she glanced at the staircase. "But the dolls…"

"Stay here. I'll go up first and let you know when to follow."

He was halfway up when he heard the moan. Signaling Cat to stay where she was, Dino took the rest of the stairs in twos. He flipped on the lights and found Jase sitting by the filing cabinets holding his head in his hands.

"What happened?" Dino asked.

"Wish the hell I knew. I let myself in the front door, reset the alarm. I came up here to check the dolls." He nodded toward the shelves. "I started at the far end and checked each one. The heads are porcelain, the bodies cloth, and there's nothing to indicate that one of them was stuffed with anything different than the others. The last thing I remember before the lights went out is something that felt like a bee sting," Jase tapped his leg. "I'm figuring whoever it was took me out with some kind of hypodermic injection." He glanced at his watch. "That was two hours ago."

"You all right?"

"Yeah. Whatever drug he or she used has worn off. The blow to my pride might take a while to heal though." He flashed Dino a grin. "Of course, catching the person who did it would be the perfect pick-me-up."

Dino glanced around the room. "Maybe he was up here when you entered, heard you and hid." Jase Campbell wasn't a man who was easily taken by surprise. "There's room behind one of those filing cabinets."

Dino looked back at the shelves where the dolls were still neatly lined up and took a quick visual count. "They're all still there."

"Perhaps because none of them contains the drugs." Jase moved to the filing cabinets. "So he hides behind one of these and lets me search all the dolls for drugs. When I get close enough, he takes me out and leaves."

"What drugs?"

Dino drew in a deep breath and turned slowly to find Cat standing at the top of the stairs, her hands on her hips, her eyes flashing. She waved a hand at Jase. "Who is this man and why did he search my dolls for drugs?"

"Cat McGuire, this is Jase Campbell, an old navy buddy of mine. He owns his own security firm now."

Her foot began to tap and she bit out each word. "Why is he searching my dolls for drugs?"

"I asked him to."

Jase eased himself up from the floor. "I think this is my cue to exit."

Cat whirled on him. "Not until I find out what's going on here."

Jase inclined his head toward Dino. "He can tell you everything. I work for him." Then he turned to Dino. "I'm going to check around, see if the coast is clear. Then I'll be back and help you get her safely to the apartment."

Giving Cat a brief nod, he strolled toward the stairs and began his descent.

"Well?" Cat asked.

Dino drew a deep breath. This wasn't the way he'd intended to tell her, but he'd known from the moment he'd pulled out his gun in the alley that the time for keeping her in the dark was over. And there was no way to sugarcoat the truth. "Your store is under investigation. It's believed that someone is using the Cheshire Cat to smuggle cocaine in from Paxco, Mexico."

9

HER HEAD STILL SPINNING, Cat paced back and forth in her office, trying to walk off her anger. Dino had insisted on seeing Jase out so that he could make sure that the place was secure. She could hardly argue with that since more than one person had evidently been making themselves at home in her store tonight.

And she needed a moment to gather herself. To think. Her first reaction to what Dino had told her had been furious denial. There was still a part of her that wanted to believe that what he'd told her was impossible. But there'd been something in his eyes that had doubt and fear surging through her.

Whirling, she faced the beautiful dolls her mother had designed. Had someone used them to smuggle drugs? She didn't want it to be true. But Dino obviously believed that it was. He'd hired a security expert to search her dolls. The image of Dino in the alley, carrying that gun as if it belonged in his hand, came to her.

Okay. That much was understandable. He'd worked in special ops. He was used to dangerous assignments. But why had he brought a gun to the job of playing her dazzled fiancé? Then she recalled his strange reaction when she'd raced out of the store to meet the FedEx man—the way he'd shoved her behind him as if he were protecting her from danger. A suspicion formed in her mind.

She strode the length of her office again. Navy Captain Dino Angelis had a lot of explaining to do. But for now, she refocused on the people who'd broken into her supposedly locked store.

She tapped her fingers. There was Jase and the man who'd knocked Jase out. Dino had claimed he'd seen two men fighting in the alley. One of them must have been Uncle Jack and he'd been wounded.

Had her uncle been in the Cheshire Cat, too?

Why? And who had been fighting with him in that alley? Not Jase. He'd been unconscious in her office.

And why hadn't anyone called the police? She strode to her desk, but she didn't reach for the phone. Because the word forming a drumbeat in the back of her mind was *drugs*.

No, it couldn't be possible. She glanced again at the dolls she'd lined up on the shelves, each one sitting on a client's order form and waiting to be placed in a Cheshire Cat gift bag. They'd been created from her mother's design. How could someone have used them to smuggle drugs?

Quickly, she strode to the shelves and one by one she examined each doll, pressing and probing. But all she felt beneath the smooth cotton was the finely milled sawdust she'd been promised. Next she tested the weight of each one in her hands. They were all exactly the same.

And they were all still here. Surely, if one of them had contained drugs, it would be missing. Jase and Dino had to be mistaken. There weren't any drugs in her dolls.

But then why had her shop been broken into? Who had hurt her uncle Jack?

Think. She wasn't an idiot. Nor could she afford to be an ostrich and bury her head in the sand. The dolls on the shelves in her shop weren't the only ones that had arrived from Paxco,

Mexico, that day. Perhaps one of the other three contained the shipment of drugs. With a sigh, Cat sank into her desk chair and dropped her head into her hands.

That was the way that Dino found her when he climbed up to the office again. Something around his heart tightened. He wanted badly to go to her, take her into his arms and just hold her. Ruthlessly, he pushed his feelings aside. That might be what she needed, but it had nothing to do with the job he'd been hired to do.

Jase was going to check out the two apartments and make sure that his man was still on duty there. Then he would come back and help him get Cat safely back into her building.

After that, Jase was going to check more thoroughly into Jack Phillips' business in Mexico. Dino planned to have a little heart-to-heart with Cat's father on the same topic.

But no steps he took now mitigated the fact that he'd been in bed with Cat while someone had broken into her store. Jase had been drugged, and from the evidence, it looked as though her uncle had been wounded.

He'd already taken too many missteps where she was concerned. Still, he would have preferred to deal with the Cat who had stood at the top of the stairs a few moments ago, her temper flaring.

As if she'd read his mind, she straightened her shoulders, rose and whirled to face him. One look at the controlled fury on her face had relief streaming through him.

"I have a few questions for you, Captain Angelis."

"Fire away."

"Who are you really working for?"

"Your father."

"But he didn't just hire you to be my fiancé for the holidays and bring peace and joy to my family until Lucia Merceri flies her broomstick back to Rome. He hardly needed a navy captain trained in special ops for that, did he?"

"I suppose not."

Her hands fisted at her sides. "I feel so stupid. I should have suspected something. But you…you totally blindsided me."

There was angry accusation in her tone, and he sympathized with it entirely. "If it's any consolation, the blindsiding was mutual."

"Not just in the line of duty?"

"No." It was in that moment that Dino decided he was going to tell her everything. Not only was it the best way to keep her safe, but she deserved the truth.

"If I'd been sticking to the line-of-duty stuff, I never should have touched you."

For a moment, there was silence in the room, but Cat's voice was still cool when she demanded, "So why did my father really hire you— -and I want it all. No more lies."

"You'd better sit down." Dino moved to the cabinet where she kept brandy and poured some into a snifter.

"How did you know I keep brandy there?"

"I searched this office while I was making the dollhouse."

"Of course you did."

When she took the snifter from his outstretched hand, Dino thought for a moment that he might end up wearing it. But she finally set it next to her on the desk and crossed her arms in front of her. "Tell me everything."

"As I said before, someone is using your shop to smuggle very high-quality cocaine from Mexico into Manhattan for an elite clientele."

When she didn't flinch, didn't argue, Dino knew with some relief that she'd already accepted the possibility.

"There's proof?"

"Enough to involve the FBI, the CIA, and Homeland Security."

Her brows snapped together. "Why Homeland Security?"

"They suspect that the profits from the smuggling are being funneled to terrorist cells in this country."

She reached for the brandy then and took a careful sip. Her hand only trembled a little, but her voice was perfectly steady. "Smuggling *and* terrorists. It just keeps getting better and better."

She began to pace. Was it only hours ago that he'd watched her do the same thing while she was trying to figure out what to do about the attraction they were feeling for each other? When she'd admitted to him that he was the only toy she wanted for Christmas.

"There have to be people involved at both ends. Do they know who?"

"They have their suspicions. According to your father, the CIA is handling the surveillance in Mexico. The feds and Homeland Security are trying not to trip over each other up here. They haven't moved yet because they don't just want to catch the people who are supplying and receiving the drugs. They want the kingpin behind the whole operation."

She stopped and turned to face him. "And they suspect someone in the Cheshire Cat is passing the drug-stuffed toys on to this kingpin?"

"Yes."

"Well, they're wrong. Adelaide and Matt love this store almost as much as I do."

Dino said nothing.

"As for Josie, well, to think that she's part of some kind of smuggling ring is ridiculous."

"People will do a lot for money. Or ideology."

Cat snorted. "Next, you'll tell me that they suspect me."

When he didn't immediately answer, she read it in his eyes. "They suspect me!"

"You're the prime suspect. But they also have their eyes on the others. Any one of your employees could be passing the drugs on. I've only spent a matter of hours here, but Josie and Adelaide know where everything is. I'll bet they both know the security code to the store. Matt, too, I'm betting. You trust them implicitly."

Her chin lifted. "Yes, I do. They're not involved in this. I'd stake my life on it."

Dino let his voice chill. "No matter how much you trust them, if you let any one of them know about this, you *are* staking your life on it."

"It's ridiculous to think that one of them would harm me."

But there was a frown in her eyes as she took another sip of the brandy. "So according to the FBI, the CIA and Homeland Security, I'm either a stupid patsy or I've decided to get a little extra excitement in my life by smuggling drugs. Who knows? Maybe I got into it to feed my own habit?"

Dino said nothing.

She glanced around the room once before meeting his eyes again. "What do you believe, Captain Angelis?"

He met her gaze steadily. "I won't lie to you. Your father believes you to be as innocent as the kind of child you cater to in this store. But originally, I had my doubts."

Her chin lifted. "And was seducing me part of your plan to clear up those doubts?"

He moved quickly then and grabbed her by the shoulders. "As I recall, the seduction was mutual. If I'd had any idea that we were going to become lovers, I never would have taken this assignment."

But hadn't he known on some level from the first time he'd looked at her photo that they were going to end up as lovers?

Dropping his hands, he took a careful step back. "If it makes any difference, I only had to be in this shop with you for half a day to know that you weren't involved."

Her eyes searched his face. "How could you be so sure?"

"You love this place. And you would never have used a doll your mother designed to smuggle drugs."

She stepped toward him then and wrapped her arms around him. Her cheek nuzzled into his neck in a gesture that he found incredibly endearing. In spite of his resolve, his arms went around her and held tight.

She should hate him for deceiving her. That might have made it easier for him to keep his hands off of her—to do his job. But each time he thought he could anticipate what she would do, she surprised him.

Dino found himself trapped again, this time not by her passion and fire, but by her vulnerability.

Finally, she lifted her head and said, "So, what are we going to do?"

He snapped his mind back to reality. "*We're* not going to do anything. I'm going to take you back to your apartment and you're going to sleep. And you're going to let Jase and me do our job."

Her eyes gleamed with determination. "The two of you haven't located the drugs yet, have you?"

"No."

"I think I know where they are." She tapped a finger against his chest. "They're in the damaged doll. All of the other dolls are the same. And anyone who knows me, would be certain that I wouldn't sell that doll to anyone."

Dino suppressed an inward sigh. That was his suspicion, too.

"This is my shop and I intend to find out who is using it to finance terrorists. You have two choices. You can work with me, or I'll work on my own."

As she took his hand and led him down the spiral staircase, he said goodbye to any hope he had of making her take a back seat while he figured out how to keep her out of trouble.

SOMETHING WAS WRONG. Dino sensed it the moment they reached Cat's apartment. For starters, there was a thin band of light seeping out beneath the door. Jase had checked out the apartment earlier, and he would have turned off all the lights. His friend had left once he'd seen them inside the front door of the building. Signaling Cat to be quiet, Dino positioned her on one side of the door and moved to the other. Then he listened for any sound.

Nothing.

"Didn't Jase check out the apartment?" Cat whispered.

Dino nodded and held out his hand for the key. Inserting it in the lock, he whispered, "You stay there until I say it's safe."

He pushed open the door and went in low. But there was no need to fan the room with his gun. A man was sitting on Cat's sofa with his feet propped on her coffee table. The Tiffany-style lamp on the table backlit him in a soft glow. He had stripped down to a bloodstained T-shirt. With one hand he was holding a pressure bandage to his right shoulder. His other hand held a lit cigar.

"Uncle Jack!"

Before Dino could stop her, Cat shot past him, but she stopped short of the coffee table. "You're hurt."

"It's just a scratch."

"I saw the blood in the snow."

"Most of that was from the other guy. He pulled a knife and sliced me, but I wrestled it away and managed to give him a taste of his own medicine."

"I'm going to get the first-aid kit." She dashed toward the bedroom, but in the doorway, she turned back. "Uncle Jack, this is my fiancé Captain Dino Angelis." Then she whirled again and was gone.

"I'd rather have a beer," Jack muttered.

Dino closed the door and leaned against it. In person, Jack Phillips looked younger than his years. He recalled Cat's description of him as a real life Peter Pan. It fit. "She doesn't have any."

"I know."

"I can offer you wine or bottled water. She may have some brandy."

"I'll pass for now." Jack met his eyes. "Why don't you put that gun away? We're on the same side."

"Are we?" Dino slipped his weapon into his jacket pocket. "Why don't you tell me what you're really doing here?"

Lowering his voice, Jack said, "I'm trying to keep my niece from getting her pretty throat slit."

"And breaking into her store is how you do that?"

Jack was saved from answering when Cat reentered the room. For the next few minutes, Dino watched Cat minister to her uncle's wound—which really was only a scratch. Evidently, the man could handle himself in a fight. A grudging admiration warred with something else as he observed the easy rapport between the two. Jealousy?

That was ridiculous. Jack Phillips was her uncle.

He had to get a grip. Whatever emotions she was pulling out of him, they were distracting him from concentrating on the job. One thing was clear. Phillips hadn't come to Cat's apartment to take advantage of her nursing skills. Dino let his gaze shift slowly around the room.

The signs were subtle, a drawer in the desk left slightly open, the shade on the window that overlooked the courtyard raised higher than when he'd seen the two men locked in that desperate struggle earlier.

Had Jack Phillips been alternately checking the courtyard while he'd been searching his niece's apartment? That's exactly what Dino would have done.

What was Jack Phillips' game? There wasn't a doubt in Dino's mind that Phillips was James McGuire's CIA informant. The question was how deeply was Cat's uncle involved in what was going on in Paxco?

"There." Cat laid a final piece of tape over her uncle's "scratch."

Then she rose and said, "Now, I want you to explain the remark you made to Dino about keeping me from getting my throat slit."

When Jack shot him a look, Dino smiled. "You might as well come clean. She knows just about everything."

"You came here to search my apartment," Cat said.

Dino shrugged. "See?"

Jack turned to Cat, a woeful expression on his face. "How can you accuse me of something like that?"

Cat crossed her arms across her chest and began to tap her foot. "I'm not a kid anymore, Uncle Jack. I saw you in that alley. The door to my shop was open, and Dino's friend Jase was taken out with a hypodermic syringe."

Jack tapped his chest with his free hand. "And you suspect *moi?*"

Cat fisted her hands on her hips. "It's more than a suspicion. Don't you remember bragging to me when I was *much* younger about special drugs that the CIA had that once injected into the victim would put him out for hours?"

Dino began to enjoy himself. He figured the score was Cat one; Jack zero.

"You might as well admit it. You were already there searching the dolls when Jase arrived—so you took him out with a hypodermic, didn't you?"

Jack shifted uncomfortably. "I'm taking the Fifth."

With a sound very much like a snort, Cat waved a hand in the direction of her tote bag. "And then there's the small matter that you moved my tote bag. Probably after you searched it. I'd already come to the conclusion that the doll with the ripped lace contained the drugs. Ask Dino."

"Shit," Jack muttered. He glanced at Dino. "They marked the doll by ripping the lace?"

"That's our current theory," Dino said. "We were about to check it out."

"I could use a drink. Maybe you could look for that brandy?"

Cat sent Dino a warning glance. "Not a chance. Don't give him a thing until he comes clean. To borrow a phrase, he's in this up to his 'pretty throat.'"

Ruffled, Jack rose to his feet. "I never thought I'd see the day when my own niece would turn against me."

"Hah!" Cat stepped toward him. "Who's turned against whom? You didn't express one iota of surprise when I introduced Dino as my fiancé." She pointed an accusing finger at her uncle. "You've been in contact with my father."

When Jack opened his mouth to protest, Cat raised one hand to cut him off.

"Don't bother to deny it. That's one of his cigars you're smoking. He's filled you in on everything, hasn't he?"

"I think it's the other way around," Dino said softly, his gaze on Jack Phillips.

Jack and Cat both turned to look at him.

"When he hired me, McGuire kept referring to his CIA informant. Since the CIA doesn't usually have the reputation of being loose-lipped, I had Jase Campbell check you out. When Cat told me that the last time you'd contacted her, you were in Mexico, it wasn't hard to put two and two together. You're running the CIA surveillance on the Paxco end of this operation, aren't you?"

Cat shifted her gaze from Dino to her uncle. "You knew my shop was being used to funnel drugs into this country and you didn't think you should tell me?"

Jack sighed. "I figured the less you knew the safer you'd be. And if the original plan had gone smoothly, it would be over. You'd be free and clear of it by now."

"I want to know everything you know, Uncle Jack." She rounded on Dino, "You, too. I won't be left in the dark about this anymore."

When Jack still hesitated, Dino said, "I'd advise you to tell her everything. Otherwise, she'll just poke around until she figures it out."

Noting that Cat's face had turned very pale, Dino moved into the kitchen, located a bottle of brandy and poured three glasses. When he'd told her about the smuggling earlier, she'd probably still entertained some hope that there was a mistake. Now it was beginning to really sink in.

"You and your father are so much alike," Jack said. "Stubborn, demanding. Why couldn't you be more like your mother?"

"Quit stalling. First, tell me everything you know about the drugs."

Dino distributed the brandy. "He knows a lot about them.

And when he found out your shop was involved, he contacted your father."

Jack glared at Dino. "Talk about loose lips."

"You and my father are actually working together on this?"

"You could say that." Jack took a good slug of the brandy.

"Then it must be serious." She shifted her gaze to Dino. "Uncle Jack and my father mix about as well as oil and water."

"It's deadly serious. That man I was fighting with in the alley was a pro." Jack glanced at Dino. "He came in just after I took out your man. I barely had time to duck back behind the cabinet. Seeing the body on the floor made him a bit wary, and his examination of the dolls was cursory. He must have known to look for the ripped lace. I didn't have a second hypodermic so I followed him out. But he must have sensed me. He jumped me the moment I stepped into the alley. He probably thought I had the doll."

"So whoever is behind this is desperate enough to hire a pro to do his or her dirty work," Dino said.

"The bastard has kept his distance right from the get-go. No one has a clue about who's running this thing. And it's not going to take a genius to figure out that if the doll containing the drugs isn't in the store, there's a good chance that Cat has it."

Jack met his niece's eyes. "You're in a pile of trouble, Cat."

10

CAT BADLY WANTED to sit down, but she kept her spine straight, her gaze steady on her uncle's. "Let's back up a bit. You mentioned an original plan. What exactly went wrong with it?"

Jack began to pace. "The whole thing was supposed to be over by now. We'd laid the perfect trap."

"We?" Cat asked.

"I have an informant who works in the place where your toys are crafted. We suspected the toys the drugs were being shipped in were one of a kind and, therefore, easily identifiable by whomever is on the receiving end up here."

"Do you know who that is?" Cat asked.

Jack shook his head. "My favorite candidate is Matt Winslow. He travels back and forth and so he's in a position to know what's going on at both ends. But my informant has never been able to definitively finger him. Which means Winslow is either innocent or very good."

"Are you usually in the store when a shipment is due to arrive?" Dino asked.

Cat nodded. "Always."

"Who else was on hand when the last shipment from Paxco arrived?" Dino asked.

Cat sipped her brandy, trying hard to bring the scene to mind. "The box arrived two weeks ago, right on schedule, shortly before noon. There were a variety of toys in the order—tin soldiers, each holding their weapon in a different position. Matt unpacked those and found a space for them on the shelves. Adelaide was excited about the drummer boy. He was two and a half feet tall. She put him on display in the window, I think." Cat sank onto the sofa.

"You're doing great," Dino said. "What else do you remember?"

"Josie oohed and aahed over the matadors. Each one had a different colored cape. And there were two dolls—Spanish dancers, one with her hair up and one with her hair down. I think she paired them up with two of the matadors and put them in the other window."

"So each toy was distinctive in some way?"

Cat nodded. "That's part of the charm."

"Do you remember which ones sold on the same day they arrived?" Dino asked.

"Right," Jack added. "The toy with the drugs is probably passed on right away."

"Or they put it aside so that it isn't sold until that person walks into the store," Dino pointed out.

"More than one sold that day. I remember wishing I'd ordered more. And there are some regular customers who stop by when they know a shipment is due. Could the person behind this be one of my regulars?"

"Possible but unlikely," Dino mused. "It would be very risky to show up in your shop regularly. And so far the person running this show has been very careful to keep his or her distance."

"So that means we're back to square one." Setting her brandy glass on the coffee table, Cat pressed her hands against her temples. "So tell me about the original trap you set, Uncle Jack."

"My informant told me that there was another order due to ship out to the Cheshire Cat the week before Christmas. We were pretty sure the man who was packing the drugs into the toy was the man who supervised the workshop."

"Juan Rivero," Cat murmured.

"Yeah. We knew exactly when the dolls were going to be shipped and we knew when they'd arrive. This time we were going to have our person in the store watching to see exactly what happened to each toy—especially the ones that were unique. That's when everything began to unravel."

"You discovered that the order was for twenty-five identical dolls," Dino said.

Jack nodded. "That was problem number one, and I didn't anticipate it. Then the drugs were late arriving in Paxco. By the time that problem was solved, the weather in the northeast was going south."

Cat rose from the sofa. "Every single one of my customers knew that they were ordering the same doll. So if the mastermind behind this is one of them, he or she was aware there would be a potential problem about identifying the doll at this end. Why run that risk? Why not wait for another shipment?"

"Never underestimate the power of greed," Jack said.

Cat recalled that Dino had used almost the same words earlier. But it was still hard for her to picture Matt or Adelaide or Josie being that hungry for money.

"They may not have had a choice. There may have been pressure from whomever is funneling the money to the terrorist cell," Dino pointed out. "Fanatics are not known for their understanding and patience."

"So they ripped the lace on the dress of one of the dolls to identify the one carrying the drugs," Cat said.

"That seems to be a likely possibility," Jack agreed. "That

way the person working on this end could easily identify it, and perhaps even offer to repair it."

"Removing the drugs in the process," Cat finished.

"Or perhaps just stretching out the repair process until the right customer walked in," Jack pointed out.

"There are a lot of ways the scenario could have played out," Dino commented.

"You got that right," Jack said. "It was a nightmare. I had five operatives set to masquerade as customers so they could try to identify the doll. It might have worked if it hadn't been for the blasted storm." Jack's tone held a wealth of bitterness.

As Jack continued to lament the string of things that had messed up his plan, Cat realized that the two men were actually enjoying their discussion—as if it were some kind of theoretical strategy game. But it wasn't. They were talking about drugs being shipped through her store.

"For starters, the shipment arrived when only Cat was in the store," Jack was complaining. "I had a man across the street ready to come into the shop the moment the delivery was made, but the prime suspects were all gone by that time. And then she closed up."

Cat had heard just about enough. "Sorry to have messed up your master plan, Uncle Jack, but Matt was stuck in Chicago, and I'd sent Adelaide and Josie home because of the weather. I hardly needed them in the store when there were no customers. So I'm the one who set aside the damaged doll. And we all know exactly where it is."

She moved behind the sofa to where she'd dropped the tote and leaned down. As she did so, she heard the sound of glass shattering behind her and in her peripheral vision, she saw the wood on the edge of her coffee table splinter. Then the breath was knocked out of her as Dino shoved her to the floor beneath the window.

"Get the lights, Phillips."

"Working on it."

Before Cat could fill her lungs with air, the room was pitched into darkness. She felt Dino pull out his gun. Then he began to ease himself off of her.

She grabbed his jacket. "Was that what I think it was?"

He pried her fingers loose. "That was a bullet aimed at you." His voice was hard, cold, and there was just enough light for her to see the flatness in his eyes. "So stay put."

Dino rose and pressed himself against the wall to the left of the window.

Cat wasn't sure she could have moved even if she wanted to. She kept hearing the glass shatter, seeing the coffee table splinter. The images played over and over like a video loop in her mind. If she hadn't bent over to pick up the tote at that particular instant…

Fisting her hands, Cat pushed the picture firmly out of her mind and focused instead on what her uncle and Dino were saying in hushed voices.

"Any idea where the shot came from?"

"Not from the ground," Dino said. "The angle's wrong. I'm betting from one of the offices above the Cheshire Cat."

"Makes sense," Jack said. "This rear window thing can work two ways."

And he should have thought of that sooner, Dino berated himself as he inched his way along the wall to the door. "I'm going to check it out. You make sure Cat stays put."

Dino punched in Jase's number even as he stepped into the hallway, then breathed a sigh of relief when his friend immediately picked up. "Tell me you're close."

"I'm still in front of Cat's building. I decided to hang around for a bit, just in case things hadn't settled down for the night."

"Someone just tried to shoot Cat through the window of her apartment."

"Is she all right?"

"Only because she chose that particular moment to stoop over and pick up her bag." He entered the stairwell and willed the image out of his mind of Cat framed in that window—the perfect target. He plunged down the steps, three at a time. He should have anticipated the danger. Should have—

Ruthlessly, Dino reined his thoughts in. He needed to think coolly. Objectively. "I'm betting the sniper took aim from one of the offices on the fourth floor over the Cheshire Cat." Pausing at the door leading to the courtyard, he scanned the windows he was referring to. Yeah, that's what he would have done. But they were all dark, all closed.

"Meet you there."

Pocketing his phone, Dino pushed through the doors and raced across the courtyard. When he stepped out of the alley, he spotted Jase standing in the doorway next to the Cheshire Cat's entrance.

"He's gone," Jase said. "I reached the corner just in time to see him dash out of here into a waiting car. By the time I got my gun out, they were more than a block away. In a hurry, though." Jase opened the door into a small foyer that offered both an elevator and access to a staircase. "He forgot to lock up."

Fear, anger and frustration roiled through him. Dino gave them a moment before he shoved them down. Then he turned to Jase. "I should have anticipated they'd try something like this."

"Why?"

Dino filled Jase in on what they'd learned from Jack

Phillips. "Whoever's behind this is getting desperate. Not only did they hire someone to break into Cat's store to get the doll, but I'm betting they also hired the thugs who tried to steal the shipment of dolls off the FedEx truck. Nothing about the operation is running the way it's supposed to. And I'm convinced that the person pulling the strings is beginning to fear exposure. At this point, they can no longer count on Cat being ignorant of what's going on in her store. And they may fear that she'll start putting two and two together and figure out which one of her employees is betraying her. I should have taken more precautions."

"Playing the blame game is never productive," Jase commented quietly.

"Right." Dino knew that. But the image was still there—of Cat framed in that window. He had to shake it loose.

"Why don't you get back to her? I'll check out the offices and let you know if I find anything."

Dino nodded and turned away. He wanted to get Cat away from this.

His need to protect her had gone far beyond the professional.

CAT AND HER UNCLE were in the kitchen when Dino returned. They'd pulled all the shades down and the only illumination in the apartment came from one of the red pillar candles they'd set on the counter. The doll lay in the space between them, its dress pulled over its head.

Jack turned to Dino immediately. "Did you get him?"

Dino shook his head. "He had a driver waiting. Jase is checking out the offices above the toy store. He's not going to find anything."

"We found something," Cat said. "This doll is definitely the one stuffed with cocaine."

She'd had to do something while she'd been waiting for Dino's return, something besides worry that he wouldn't. Her uncle had tried to soothe her by pointing out that the pro had been hired to get her, not Dino.

Small comfort that was. Just as it was small comfort to know that the doll in front of her actually contained smuggled cocaine. Her stomach did a quiet, long flip. She was beginning to realize that theory was one thing and reality was quite another.

When Dino placed his hand on her shoulder, she glanced at him. The understanding she saw in his eyes helped her to gather her strength. She finally asked the question that had been on her mind since he'd left. "Why does someone want to kill me? That wouldn't necessarily get them the doll and the drugs."

"They may be afraid that you're going to start putting two and two together and get four," Dino said. "So far you've been the innocent dupe, but this time things are going wrong on both ends of the operation. If there's even a chance that you know about the drugs, they might figure it's not going to take you long to figure out who's betraying you, and that person could bring our kingpin down."

"Plus, they may have felt that in the confusion of dealing with your untimely demise, they might have a chance to snatch the doll," Jack said.

Cat glanced down at the doll. "So the question is what do we do next?"

"*We're* not going to do anything," Jack said. "You're going to leave this up to your fiancé and me."

"When hell freezes over," Cat said. But whatever else she would have said was interrupted when her cell phone rang. Setting the doll aside, she dug the phone out of her purse and checked the caller ID. Her father.

"Dad? Is something wrong?"

"What's wrong is that you're not answering your cell. I've been trying to reach you for almost an hour."

Cat glanced at the two men who'd moved into the living room. No doubt to develop new strategies. Well, she had an idea or two of her own. "Things have been busy here."

"Busy? You close your store at 8:00."

"Thanks to you, I have a fiancé to deal with now."

There was a beat of silence on the other end of the line. "How is that going?"

"Fine." Cat briefly considered letting her father know that she was fully aware of what was going on in her store. What would he say if she told him that she had a doll stuffed with cocaine sitting on her kitchen counter and that someone had just taken a shot at her?

A glance into the dim living room told her that Dino and Jack had their heads close together, talking in low tones. The last thing she needed was another person strategizing how to keep her safely on the sidelines while the big strong men brought down the drug ring.

"Dad, what was so urgent that you needed to get in touch with me?"

McGuire cleared his throat. "I know it's late, but I had to make sure you knew. Lucia's plane made it into LaGuardia before it closed down, and she announced at dinner tonight that she intends to visit your store tomorrow."

Cat's stomach knotted. "Tomorrow? Absolutely not. Now that the weather's cleared up, do you have any idea how busy we'll be?"

Images of chaos flooded Cat's mind. Twenty-two customers were going to be picking up their dolls. The mastermind behind the drug ring or one of his hired minions was going to looking for the doll with the torn lace. Uncle Jack's men were going to be in and out of the store hoping to make an arrest.

And in the midst of all that, she pictured Lucia Merceri, cane in hand, thumping her way through the store with the single-minded intention of grilling Dino.

Out of the corner of her eye, Cat could see that Dino was also on his cell—probably checking in with Jase. More plans were being made, she thought. Without consulting her. The little flame of anger that had been burning inside of her ever since that sniper had shot at her flared hotly.

"We won't stay long," her father promised.

Liar, Cat thought. How long they stayed would depend entirely on Lucia. "Just tell the Queen of Hearts she'll have plenty of time to get to know Dino at the ball tomorrow night."

"Don't you think I tried? Lucia claims there will be too much going on at a big charity event like that. And there'll be others demanding her attention. Your stepsister Lucy and her husband weren't able to make it for dinner tonight because of the storm. Besides, Lucia's heard so much about Dino that she can't wait to meet him. If it hadn't been for the weather, she would have visited your shop today."

Cat badly wanted to scream, but there were better ways of handling her father. "Daddy, you can talk her out of it, I know you can. Tell her we'll stop by the house before the ball. She can have some private time with Dino. Believe me, there won't be an inch of space in my shop tomorrow."

"I have no control over the situation. Plus, Gianna is bringing a dress she wants you to wear to the ball. She knows you haven't had any time to shop. It's two against one, little girl."

Right. Cat bit down hard on her tongue. "What time?"

Her father sighed. "About ten. I knew you'd understand."

"Oh, I do." What she understood was her father wanted to

poke his nose into the Cheshire Cat, too. He was probably tired of getting secondhand reports from Jack and Dino. Grimly, Cat accepted the fact that if she didn't fill her father in on what was going on, Dino or her Uncle Jack would.

"Would you like to talk to Uncle Jack?"

"I thought Jack was in Mexico."

"When I walked into my apartment tonight, he was sitting on my sofa smoking one of your cigars. I know that the two of you have been plotting together."

"I don't know what—"

"Give it up, Dad. My store was broken into tonight, and Uncle Jack fought with the burglar. And by the way, I know why you really hired Dino Angelis."

"Cat—"

"I don't appreciate being lied to. See you in the morning."

"Now wait—"

Cat dropped her cell back into her tote, then turned to study the two men in the dim shadows of her living room. So far everyone had been operating around her, keeping her in the dark. Her father, hiring a bodyguard in the guise of a fake fiancé, her uncle, joining forces with her father to catch a drug smuggler who was using her shop and her mother's dolls to finance terrorists.

And no one had thought she'd had a right to know?

Right now, she could tell that Dino and her uncle were hatching some plot to sideline her again.

In a pig's eye.

As CAT STRODE forward to join them, Dino turned. Since it was Jack's plan, he was going to let Cat's uncle break the news. And take the grief.

"You've come up with a plan."

Dino noted that it wasn't a question.

"Here's how it's going to go down," Jack said.

Cat's chin lifted, but she held her tongue.

"You're not going into the store tomorrow. Dino will tell your employees you spent the night in the emergency room— some kind of twenty-four-hour bug—and that he didn't have the heart to wake you up. That's the story your customers will hear. In the meantime, you'll be in the apartment next door with Jase Campbell, and one of my men will be here. When someone breaks in this place to find the doll, we'll have them."

"That's it?" Cat asked in a mild voice.

"Yes."

She moved until she was standing toe to toe with her uncle. Then she poked a slim finger into his chest. "That's a very interesting scenario, but we're not using it."

"Cat—"

She cut Jack off by poking him again. "For starters, Lucia Merceri, accompanied by my father and Gianna, are coming to the Cheshire Cat tomorrow morning at ten. Daddy claims he's outnumbered by the women, and has no control over the situation, and Lucia can't wait another minute to meet and cross-examine my fiancé."

"I'll call your father and talk to him," Jack said.

"Won't do you a bit of good. Wild horses wouldn't keep him away from my store tomorrow. I filled him in on what happened tonight. The part about the store being broken into. I didn't tell him someone tried to shoot me." She shot a look at Dino. "But I told him that I know my fake fiancé is really my bodyguard."

"Shit," Jack muttered.

"Even if you did talk Dad out of coming to the store, Lucia Merceri is a force of nature. The only thing that stopped her from coming today was the blizzard. I'm not leaving Dino alone to deal with her. And even if you did talk me into playing sick, the wicked witch would be over here in a flash. Dino isn't the only one she'll have questions for. If we go with your plan, my apartment stands a good chance of becoming Grand Central Station."

"I don't want you in the shop." Jack turned to Dino. "Tell her how much danger she's in."

"She already knows." Dino kept his eyes on Cat as she turned away from her uncle and began to pace in and out of the shadows. He knew her well enough now to recognize that she was thinking something through—in much the same way she'd thought her little proposition through just before she'd sprung it on him. Resting his hip against the small desk, he waited.

"The other problem with your plan, Uncle Jack, is that it has 'trap' written all over it. Dino's right—whoever's been running this operation is smart. The man you tangled with in the alley has probably already reported in. I think it's safe to say that the kingpin knows the store and my apartment are both under surveillance."

She was right about that, Dino thought. The alleyway and courtyard that connected the two buildings had been a very busy place tonight.

"Plus, my employees and my regular customers know that I'm always in the shop. Now, one of them knows or strongly suspects I have the doll with the drugs and suddenly I'm sick? No. Your plan isn't going to work."

Jack ran a hand through his hair, then glanced at Dino. "Can't you talk some sense into her?"

Cat whirled to face her uncle. "No, he can't. Someone has been using my store and one of the dolls my mother designed to smuggle filthy drugs into the country. And so far they've been able to do it very easily and with impunity. I want to catch the bastard. And I think I have a better plan than yours."

Jack sent Dino a pleading look. "C'mon, I need some backup here."

"I want to hear what she has to say," Dino said.

Cat smiled then. "I'm going to tempt whoever's behind this. When I open the Cheshire Cat tomorrow, I'll put this doll in one of the windows. She'll have a Sold tag on her arm, and I'll make sure that the torn lace is just visible. She'll be right there in plain sight."

Jack frowned. "You think someone may make a grab for it."

"No. That would be too dangerous. And just plain dumb. No one involved in this has been stupid so far." She began to pace. "I think one of my employees has to be involved. If they don't already know that the shipment has arrived, they will the moment they get to the store. I'll fill them in, tell them that Mr. Miller and Mrs. Lassiter have already picked up their dolls and that I've notified everyone else. I'll also tell them that I've put the damaged doll in the window so that we can take new orders. All day long it will be there right within reach. I want to toy with their minds. Someone may be tempted into revealing himself or herself. But I think they'll bide their time."

Dino began to wonder if Cat remembered they were there as she continued, "That's what I'd do. We're closing early tomorrow. Matt, Adelaide and Josie will all be attending the ball. I'm leaving at 5:00 because Gianna insists that I stand in the reception line. Adelaide and Josie will close the store an hour later. I'll make sure that they know that I'm taking the doll with me when I leave, that I intend to surprise my father with it at the ball."

For a moment, the two men regarded her in silence.

Then Jack scowled at her. "If you take the doll, someone will make a move on you at the ball."

Cat smiled. "Exactly. They'll think they'll have a better chance there."

"And they will," Jack said. "You're using yourself as bait, and I don't like it."

"If they don't think they have a good enough chance, they won't go for it," Cat insisted. "And if they don't feel they can make a move—a successful one—soon, whoever is behind this will probably cut his or her losses and walk away. We'll have lost our chance to catch them."

Dino waited three beats before he said, "She's right. Someone is going to believe that the ball is his or her best chance." He didn't like it—but the trap she was baiting had a better chance of succeeding than the one Jack had described. What he didn't say, what he didn't even want to think about was that catching the people behind the operation might be the only way to protect Cat's life.

He met her eyes. "I don't think your father could have come up with a better plan."

Jack turned to Dino. "You're not going to go along with this?"

"I'm not saying I like it," Dino said. "But I think she's right. No one will try and grab the doll in the store—at least not as soon as she lets everyone know she'll be taking it to the charity event. The ball opens up a lot of seemingly safer possibilities."

"Too many," Jack said.

"Enough to tempt someone to come out in the open," Cat said. "They won't be able to resist. It's the best chance we've got."

"She's right." Dino turned to Jack. "Between us, we ought to be able to come up with enough people to keep her covered. I'll be with her in the store all day—and at the ball. Jase can rotate some of his men through the store. What about you?"

"I've got the ones I was going to use for the original plan."

"Use them now for the ball."

Dino turned to Cat. "You're exhausted and you have a long day tomorrow. Get some sleep while your uncle and I hammer out the details."

"I'll need to know about them."

Dino moved toward her then and ran a hand down her arm. "We'll brief you in the morning. If this is going to work, you're going to have to put on the performance of your life tomorrow. Not only in the store, but also at the ball. That means you're going to have to be on your toes every moment. Get some rest."

IT WAS AFTER MIDNIGHT when the phone rang. The damp hand that picked the receiver up nearly dropped it.

"Do you have the doll?"

"Not yet. I called the number you gave me and made the arrangements, but the doll with the torn lace wasn't in the shop."

"Where is it?"

There was steeliness in the tone that chilled the blood.

"She must have it. It makes sense that she wouldn't sell a damaged product to anyone. She's probably repairing it."

There were three beats of silence on the other end of the line.

"You've delayed me again. The man who caused the drugs to be delayed in reaching Paxco no longer works for me. He met with an accident."

Fear surged up. "I can still get it for you. She'll be in the store all day tomorrow. I'll be able to pin down the doll's location. Give me until tomorrow night."

"We'll see. I have others who are more efficient than you."

"No! No—I'll get it."

The line went dead.

RAGE BUBBLED UP. There'd been too many failures. The robbery hadn't been successful, colleagues were beginning to panic, and Cat McGuire was still alive. The worst news was that there'd been two men in her apartment when the sniper had taken his unsuccessful shot. If Cat McGuire was being protected, there was a good chance she'd become suspicious. That meant time was running out.

Why was everyone so incompetent?

Think. There's still time.

The increasing risk of exposure would have to be dealt with. Quickly. Perhaps depending so much on others had been a mistake….

11

IT WAS JUST AFTER THREE when Jack finally left to return to his hotel. After locking the door of Cat's apartment, Dino glanced at the sofa where he was going to spend the rest of the night. Cat needed her sleep, and he knew if he joined her in bed, neither of them would get much.

The plan that he and Jack had come up with to keep Cat safe at the ball was a good one. Still, Dino had a feeling—the same kind of feeling that had plagued him on his last special ops mission. Something was going to go wrong. He pressed his hands against his eyes, then dropped them.

The trick was to keep Cat safe, but at the same time offer someone the opportunity to snatch the doll. Once he'd accepted the fact that his niece wasn't going to be sidelined, Jack had proven himself to be a good strategist. Since Matt, Josie and Adelaide were all still under suspicion, they'd come up with two plans. Each left Cat vulnerable for a time.

If Matt was the one who was receiving and passing on the drugs, he'd try to get Cat alone at some point during the charity ball. They'd have to let him succeed—at least until he incriminated himself.

The most obvious place for one of the women to isolate Cat was in the ladies' room, so Jase would station a woman operative there for the entire evening.

Jack had volunteered to bring Cat's father up to date first thing in the morning.

Dino surveyed Cat's living room. There was very little likelihood that Cat was in danger from any more snipers—at least for tonight. He and Jack had patched the section of window that the bullet had shattered. The shades were drawn, and the only light came from the red candle now burning on the coffee table.

He glanced at it, thought of the picnic they'd shared earlier and of how they'd made love right there on the floor. Had it only been nine hours ago? So much had happened since then. He picked up the candle and was on his way to the bedroom to check on Cat when his cell vibrated in his pocket. Alarm moved through him. If Jase was calling him at this hour...

Setting the candle back down, he pulled his phone out and smiled the moment he saw the caller ID. It was his cousin Kit. "Do you know what time it is?"

"It's just after midnight—the witching hour here in San Francisco. I'm up in the tower room with your mom."

Worry snaked its way up Dino's spine. He could picture them both quite clearly. Kit would be lounging on one of the comfortable sofas and his mother would probably be at her desk with her crystals spread out in front of her. After his father and aunt had died, everyone had moved into his grandfather's huge mansion. Its tower room was one of those special places on the estate where his mother's visions were strongest. The room itself was large and airy with long, narrow stained glass windows. On a clear night, she'd crank them open and let the moonlight pour into the room.

"Something wrong?" Dino asked. Of all his cousins, Kit, the novelist and PI, was the one closest to his mom.

"You tell us. Your mom is a bit worried, but she didn't want to make you worry even more. I'm thinking if you're in some kind of trouble, I could fly out there and act as backup. Theo is in court this week. But he wouldn't be much use to you anyway what with his wedding in five days. And Nik's too busy honeymooning in Greece. You'll have to make do with me."

Dino sank onto the arm of the sofa and stretched out his legs. "Has Mom seen something?"

"I'll let you talk to her."

"Dino?" His mother sounded tense.

"I'm fine, Mom."

"Yes. I've seen danger, but not for you. It's for the woman you're guarding. Someone is trying to kill her."

"Tried and failed."

"They'll try again."

Fear knotted in Dino's stomach. Hadn't his own feelings told him that? "Yes. But I won't let it happen."

"You're going to have to trust her. She's smart. She'll figure out a way when the time comes."

Some of his own tension eased at her words. "This may all be over sooner than I expected. I may be home if not for Christmas at least for Theo's wedding."

"Yes, I think you will. Bring her with you."

"I will." It wasn't until that moment that he acknowledged to himself that taking Cat to San Francisco to meet his family was something he very much wanted to do. "Tell Kit I appreciate his offer to fly out here, but I have some very good backup already—Jase Campbell, a man I worked special ops with in the navy."

"Kit will be disappointed," Cass said with a smile in her voice. "But I told him he wasn't going to escape that easily from the wedding preparations. Take care, Dino."

"I will."

Even after he pocketed his cell, Dino continued to sit on the arm of the sofa. For the first time since the bullet had shattered the window and missed Cat by inches, he felt that he was going to be able to protect her. He had to. Jase had been right that playing the blame game was only going to interfere with his instincts. And he was going to need every bit of the power that ran in his family during the next twenty-four hours.

Had his mother somehow sensed that? Of course. A sudden wave of longing moved through him. He wanted to see her and just be with his family. He glanced toward the bedroom door. But he also wanted to be with Cat. Just how he was going to resolve that he hadn't quite worked out yet.

Lifting the candle, he strode to the bedroom door and eased it open. She slept on her side with one hand tucked under her chin. She'd kicked off most of the covers and the oversized white T-shirt she wore just skimmed her thighs. One of those incredibly long legs was under the sheet, the other on top. It occurred to him that he hadn't seen her sleep before. It was hard to believe, but they hadn't known each other long enough for that. Though he might have imagined it, he'd never seen that glorious hair spread across a pillow. In the candlelight, the hint of flames that always seemed to flicker in the strands looked real.

She seemed to throw herself into sleep with the same single-minded determination that she threw herself into her work. Into lovemaking.

Because he simply couldn't help himself, Dino moved closer. From the first, she'd had the power to draw him like a magnet. He'd made a decision to keep his distance until this was over. He needed his objectivity, to keep his mind on the job. And if his mother was right, Cat needed to focus on keeping herself safe, too.

But his desire for her, the consuming need he had no control over wouldn't let him stop until he was at the side of the bed. This close, for the first time he noticed how delicate her features were, how slender her wrists. In sleep, there was a fragility to her that he hadn't noted before. Perhaps because the intense energy that seemed to emanate from her during every waking moment was absent now. She was so smart, so strong, with a mind every bit as agile as her body. She'd handled her uncle Jack just as easily as she'd handled him. She'd come up with her own plan for tomorrow and had neatly shoehorned them into it.

For the first time as he looked at her, it wasn't the hot stir of passion that he felt, but something quieter, warmer. Admiration, certainly, but also affection. It was then that he felt his heart go into freefall, and something bordering on fear moved through him.

When had it happened? When had he fallen in love with her? That first morning when he'd stood outside her store and witnessed her race down those stairs? Or had it been when he'd first seen her picture on his admiral's desk?

Setting the candle on her nightstand, he brushed a strand of hair behind her ear, felt that warm skin. It was only as she stirred that he realized he'd wanted her to wake up. Needed her to.

Her eyes opened and he watched them clear. She smiled at him and held out her hand. "Come to bed."

"It wouldn't be smart."

She levered herself up. "Here's the deal. Tomorrow we'll be smart. Tonight there's just you and me."

He stripped off his clothes, then joined her in the bed and helped her rid herself of hers.

She slipped her arms around him then and found his mouth. He kept the pressure light, remembering the tenderness he'd felt as he'd watched her sleep. He'd never been a particularly gentle lover, but she'd unlocked something inside of him.

Her lips were warm and soft as they moved over his. Her taste, her scent were so familiar now, as if they'd become a part of him. As they lingered, tasted, teased and took from each other, an ache, sweet and edgy, streamed through him. He was hers.

"Make love with me," she whispered against his lips.

"I am." With his mouth still nibbling hers, he threaded his fingers through her hair. Cat felt as if her body were melting molecule by molecule. Though she wanted to touch him, her limbs seemed weighted. A riot of sensations, sweet and bubbly as champagne moved through her. She wanted to indulge in each one—the flavor of his lips, the texture of his skin as his cheek brushed against hers. That dark penetrating gaze as he drew back to comb his hands through her hair again and again.

Then at last he touched her, fingertips only, tracing her face, rubbing her lower lip with his thumb, and circling her breasts. What was he doing to her? She'd felt his strength before, but this was different. His fingers didn't grip, his hands didn't press. Instead, they skimmed and lingered. So different. So intense. It wasn't fire he stirred in her this time, but a flood of emotions.

She watched the flicker of candlelight on his features. Those strong warrior cheekbones, the firm chin. And those eyes. She could read his desire in them, feel it in her bones. She ran her fingers over his face, absorbing, memorizing. Drawing his mouth to hers, she traced his lips with her tongue. Then she eased back and just looked and looked. This might be the last time, the very last time, they held each other like this.

His heart began to beat faster, the pulse of it matching her own. They both moved this time until their mouths met again and fused. Mists of pleasure swamped her as the ache in her throat built and built. She was vaguely aware that he took care of the condom, then linked his fingers with hers.

He said her name—only that—as he slipped into her. What she was feeling erupted and poured out and into him as they began to move. She was his.

Need turned suddenly sharper. Hands gripped, fingers dug in and they clung to one another. Greed replaced tenderness with a speed that devastated them both. Wrapped tight, they rolled across the bed, fighting to take each other further than they'd ever gone before.

Finally, he rose over her so that he was all she saw, all she knew. He drove into her almost violently and she met him thrust for thrust. His chest was heaving, as was hers. And still he held back, as if he wanted to keep them balanced, trembling on that edge—forever. Then his mouth crushed hers, and she heard only the sounds of their mingled moans as they poured themselves into each other.

IN THE MORNING, one of Jase's men drove them from the underground garage of her building into the alley by the side of the shop. Dino got out first, opened the door to the storeroom, turned on the lights and then came back to hustle Cat inside.

He took her hands in his. "Nervous?"

"A bit." It was the first time that morning that he'd touched her.

When she'd awakened, she'd been alone in her bed, the sheets next to her cold. Through the open bedroom door she'd caught a glimpse of Dino in the kitchen talking to her uncle. He was definitely back in bodyguard mode.

Trying not to feel hurt, she'd dressed comfortably for the long day ahead of her. The red sweater was for the season and the black pants and boots were to allow her maximum ease of movement. When she'd joined Dino and her uncle in the kitchen, the two men had been all business, briefing her carefully on the game plan for the day. Their eyes had been hard, their tone of voice flat and clipped. It had been the first time she'd noticed any similarities in the two men.

The plan had been simple and straightforward. And as it sunk in, nerves had knotted in her stomach. With no advance notice to her coworkers, she was going to leave the store two hours before closing at 4:00 p.m. And she was not going to return to her apartment.

"No sense in giving some sniper a second chance," Jack had said grimly. "I've reserved a suite at the Alsatian Towers where your stepmother's ball is taking place. Both of you will have to pack and take your ball clothes to the Cheshire Cat. Then you can dress in the hotel suite."

"Jase has arranged for a limo to pick us up in front of the store," Dino had added. "We'll go directly to the hotel. This is the weakest part of the plan. We're assuming that whoever is behind this will have been informed by then that you're taking the damaged doll to the ball. So once we get into the limo, they'll know our destination. To keep them from trying something then, Jase's man will drop us off at the delivery entrance and we'll use service elevators to get to the suite."

"Once you arrive at the ball, we'll have someone within three feet of you at all times. Jase's female op will be on duty in the ladies' room when you need a bathroom break," Jack had explained. "If someone makes a move on you, we'll have him."

Hopefully, she'd thought. But she hadn't said a word out loud. Odd that listening to the meticulousness of their plan hadn't eased her nerves. But now just the pressure of Dino's hands on hers had most of her anxiety draining away.

"Want a piece of advice?" Dino asked.

"Sure."

"For every move you make today, everything you say, you're going to have an audience. So think of yourself as an actress with a part to play. It's a technique I often use when I'm working a mission. It helps me focus and allows me to keep personal emotions under control and to stay objective."

Cat couldn't prevent the thought from slipping into her mind again. Was that what he'd been doing the whole time he'd been with her—playing a role? Was that what he was doing now? Quickly, she pushed the idea aside. The part she had to play didn't allow for that kind of speculation. Tilting her head slightly, she managed a smile. "I think I'll imagine myself to be a young Kate Hepburn."

He studied her for a moment. "Good choice."

He would have released her then, but she tightened her grip on his hands. "What if our plan doesn't work?"

He met her eyes. "It will. And when this is over, we'll talk."

Something moved through her—a mix of anticipation and fear…and something else she couldn't put a name to. Whatever it was, it had her heart making a good, hard thump.

"Ready?" Dino asked.

"Yes."

He pulled her close for a quick, possessive kiss. And there was no audience. Only the two of them.

"Break a leg," he murmured.

Turning, Cat moved onto her stage, crossed to one of the windows and baited her trap with the doll.

"JUST A SEC." The phone call from Matt came at nine-forty-five and had Cat scurrying to the second step of the spiral staircase to get the best signal. After pressing her cell to one ear, she cupped her palm over the other to block out the cacophony of noise that filled the store. Not even the rock version of "Jingle Bells" pouring through the speakers could completely drown out the sound of children's laughter and the din of conversation. "Matt?"

"I'm here."

"Go ahead. I can hear you now. Where are you?"

"I'm on my way in from LaGuardia." A wealth of disgust and exhaustion laced his tone. "They didn't open up the New York area airports until six this morning. I would have called earlier except we were circling, waiting for clearance to land for two hours. I should be at the Cheshire Cat within fifteen minutes. How's business?"

"Booming. We can definitely use your help." Cat kept her voice cheerful and excited as she glanced around the packed store. The bell over the door jangled and two more customers began to push their way through the crowd. She recognized them immediately. They were here to pick up their special dolls from Paxco. Earlier she'd brought them down from the office, and they were lined up next to gift bags on a shelf. Josie had taken over the distribution.

The door jangled again to let in three more people. It was as if shoppers were determined to make up for the time the blizzard had stolen from them the day before.

"Just wanted to let you know I'm on my way. I won't keep you. See you soon."

Cat stared down at her cell after Matt disconnected the call. He hadn't even asked about the shipment of dolls. Did that mean that he already knew they'd arrived? How? He hadn't been in touch with her since yesterday. But he had been tracking them on his Palm Pilot she remembered.

Then she shifted her gaze to Adelaide and Josie. She'd explained about the doll in the window display the moment they'd arrived in the shop, and they'd taken it in stride. No questions. Josie had offered to mend the ripped lace. Cat had declined her offer, explaining that she would take care of it later. For the life of her, she hadn't read anything in her eyes other than a desire to be helpful. Adelaide had merely stepped behind the counter to ring up a waiting customer. Cat wondered which behavior she should view as more suspicious. It was fortunate she'd gone into the toy business. She surely wouldn't make a very good detective.

And it made her both sad and angry to know that in less than twenty-four hours she'd gone from defending her employees to firmly believing that one of them had betrayed her.

But this wasn't the time to be reflecting on that. She had a role to play.

Pushing herself to her feet, she let her gaze sweep the store again. A few yards away to her right, Dino was crouched down next to a boy of about five, their dark heads close as they watched a train chug slowly up a steep hill. The thought slipped into her mind that he looked just right sitting on the floor of her store playing with a child. Something tightened around her heart. Unable to resist, Cat joined the man and the boy and murmured in a voice only Dino could hear, "Working hard, I see."

Dino sent her a bland look. "I'm providing a distraction while Mom shops."

Together they watched the train crest the hill. The little boy squealed and clapped his hands as it shot down the other side. Then Dino said, "There's something you should know. I asked Jase to run a check on Mrs. Lassiter and your Santa Claus man, Mr. Miller."

"Because they were so prompt picking up their dolls?"

"And because both of them had access to the tracking number and could have been involved in the attempted robbery of the FedEx truck. Mrs. Lassiter seems okay. Her husband is a very successful plastic surgeon with offices on Park Avenue. They don't seem to want for money. But the address Miller gave on his order form is the same as the Frick Museum on East 70th Street."

Cat put a hand on his arm. "He's our man?"

"Could be."

Something tugged at the edges of Cat's mind. "You know, from the moment he walked into the store, there was something familiar about him. At the time, I chalked it up to the fact that he looked a bit like Santa Claus." She met Dino's eyes. "But maybe it was more than that. I'm going to have to think about it."

"You do that." He squeezed her hand. "How's it going so far?"

"I've decided that good actresses don't get paid nearly enough."

Dino's laughter blended with the jangle of the bell over the door. Cat turned in time to see her father, Gianna, and Lucia Merceri enter. "Uh-oh, here they come."

Lucia was in the lead. The woman might be short, but she emanated a power and authority that had other customers stepping aside as she arrowed her way like a heat-seeking missile toward Cat.

Behind the parade, Cat saw Mrs. Lassiter and Matt Winslow both enter the store. Matt stepped to the window where the doll was displayed while Mrs. Lassiter pushed her way straight toward Adelaide at the counter. Cat knew a moment of panic as Matt leaned closer to the doll. Was he just going to snatch it, stuff it under his coat and run?

Keeping her hand in his, Dino rose with Cat. "Relax. Jase has it covered."

Cat had time to register that Jase had entered the shop seconds before Lucia reached them.

"Act Two begins," Dino murmured.

12

"So this is the fiancé?" Lucia demanded.

"Now, Mama Merceri, you know it is," Colonel McGuire said. "I showed you his picture."

Lucia glared at the colonel as she thumped her cane on the floor. "Does that mean I don't rate a formal introduction?"

"Of course not." Dino took Lucia's free hand and raised it to his lips. "I'm Dino Angelis, Signora Merceri. It's my pleasure to meet you. You also, Mrs. McGuire. Cat has spoken of you both."

"Humph," Lucia said, then pinned Cat with a look. "At least *he* has some manners. You're looking tired, young lady. Gianna says they never see you. High time you stopped working so hard."

She shifted her gaze back to Dino. "Checked you out. You're an old-fashioned Greek man. Maybe you can persuade her to get off this retail treadmill."

"Cat has a mind of her own. I don't believe I'll have much luck with talking her out of doing something she loves, something she's obviously so good at."

"My son-in-law says you're retiring from the navy."

"Because I want to. Not because someone pressured me into it."

"Humph." Lucia studied him for a moment. "Taking her side, are you?"

"Yes, ma'am."

Out of the corner of her eye, Cat saw that Mrs. Lassiter was first in line at Adelaide's counter and she was gesturing towards the display window. Matt hadn't touched the doll.

"The Cheshire Cat is very busy today, Signora Merceri," Dino said. "Why don't I give you and the colonel and Mrs. McGuire a tour while Cat deals with her customers?"

"That would be lovely." Gianna sent him a grateful smile.

"A little maneuver to take us off her hands," Lucia said.

Dino smiled at her as he tucked her hand into the crook of his arm. "Cat was right. She said that you'd see right through it. But since you've come all this way, you really ought to get the grand tour. First, I'd like you to meet my friend Tommy."

Cat stared for a moment as Lucia Merceri, the wicked witch, took time to acknowledge the introduction to the little boy Dino had been playing with. Then she remembered her role and hurried over to Adelaide.

Matt stepped into her path when she was halfway there. "I was wondering how you would handle the doll that didn't meet our quality control standards. I hoped to be here when the shipment arrived so that I could explain why I told Juan he could put it in. It was either that or the shipment would have been short a doll."

Cat studied her assistant buyer as he spoke. She'd never seen him look so disheveled before. And there was something in his eyes that went beyond fatigue. Was it fear?

Or was she just being paranoid about everyone who worked for her?

Guilt moved through her as she put a hand on Matt's arm. "I would have made the same decision. And it isn't a problem. I never mentioned it to you, but I ordered one of the dolls myself as a surprise Christmas gift for my father."

Matt's gaze shifted to her family. "I wondered why your family was here."

Dino had steered Lucia around the shop and was now escorting her into the storeroom. Gianna and her father were bringing up the end of the little parade.

"Do you want me to clean the doll up so that it's all set to go when they leave?" Matt asked.

"No. I'm planning on giving it to my dad tonight at Gianna's big charity ball. I figure she'll take care of the repairs."

It suddenly occurred to her that Matt didn't know about her engagement yet. Panic fluttered in her stomach, and her admiration for professional actresses and undercover agents shot up another notch.

Shoving her nerves aside, Cat beamed a smile at Matt. "They're here because Gianna's mother has made a trip over from Italy to meet my fiancé, Dino Angelis. He's giving them a tour of the shop to keep them out of my hair."

Matt stared at her. "You're engaged? Since when?"

Cat showed him her ring. "Dino proposed a week ago when we were skating at Rockefeller Center. We've been seeing each other secretly for a couple of months now. I didn't tell anyone because I figured if word leaked out to my family that I was dating someone seriously, Gianna would have been all over me. You know how much she wants me to marry and spend more of my time serving on boards and following in her footsteps. And Lucia is right with her on that."

Matt gave his head a little shake as if to clear it. "Who is this Dino Angelis?"

"Long story." And she was saved from telling it when Adelaide waved frantically for her to come over to the counter where Mrs. Lassiter's voice was on the rise. "Tell you later."

She took two steps before she turned back. "Would you mind helping Josie out until things slack off a bit?"

Relief streamed through her as Matt headed toward Josie, but it drained away when she reached Adelaide and saw the worry in her eyes.

"Mrs. Lassiter insists on buying the doll in the window," Adelaide said. "I've explained to her that it's only there for display purposes, so that we can take more orders."

"I'll give you twice what I paid for the other doll." Mrs. Lassiter's voice carried enough to have several customers joining the small crowd already gathered in front of Adelaide's work station.

Cat read both distress and determination in Mrs. Lassiter's eyes. Did the older woman know about the drugs? Was that why she wanted the doll? "I'm sorry, I can't sell you that doll. I ordered it as a gift for my father because it was created from a design my mother made. Besides, it's slightly damaged. We can certainly take your order for another doll."

Mrs. Lassiter waved a hand. "What about one of those on the shelves over there?"

There were three left, Cat saw. "They're already sold. There are children who are expecting them under the tree."

"You don't understand. I need another doll." Tears flooded Mrs. Lassiter's eyes.

She wasn't after the drugs, Cat decided. Any of the dolls would do.

Over Mrs. Lassiter's shoulder, Cat saw Josie slip one of the remaining dolls into a gift bag and the woman she passed it to clutched it to her body and headed straight for the door.

"Mrs. Lassiter, why don't you come with me?" Cat led the way to a less crowded space near the storeroom.

"Why do you need two dolls?"

The older woman took a deep breath. "My daughter-in-law just informed me that I have to give the exact same present to both Giselle and Charlene. They're only a year apart and they're beginning to fight over everything. She won't let me give Giselle the doll from Paxco unless I have one for Charlene. And I promised Giselle that doll."

Cat thought hard. She didn't have to be an ace detective to handle a panicked grandmother. "Didn't you buy the bride doll with the fashion trunk and accessories for Charlene?"

"Yes."

"I have another one of those over here." She led the way to a display table and squatted down to find the box. Thank heavens, they'd been too busy lately to keep up with unpacking everything. "Why don't you give the bride dolls to Giselle and Charlene for Christmas and wait for their birthdays to give them the dolls from Paxco? I should be able to get another shipment in by the end of January."

"I suppose I could do that," Mrs. Lassiter said. "Giselle's birthday is in early February."

"That isn't a very long time to wait."

Taking the bride doll box, Mrs. Lassiter met her eyes just before she turned away. "Thank you, Ms. McGuire. I think you've saved the day."

"Nice work."

Cat whirled to find Dino standing just behind her. She sent a panicked look over his shoulder. "My family? Is everything all right?"

He grinned at her. "Everything's fine. I made coffee for each of them and Lucia is presently on the phone talking to my mother."

Cat stared at him. "She's talking to your mother?"

"Claimed she was interested in meeting the whole family.

She even mentioned a trip to San Francisco. But from what I could tell the conversation is turning into a consultation. When Lucia ran a background check on me, she discovered my mother's reputation as a psychic. And Lucia is curious about her future."

Cat put a hand on his arm. "But your mother doesn't even know about the engagement."

Dino linked his fingers with hers. "Relax. I spoke with her earlier, but she probably knew we were going to meet and become involved before we did. I want you to meet her." Dino hadn't known he was going to say that, hadn't known the words were true until they were spoken.

He saw the immediate flash of nerves in Cat's eyes, felt her fingers slip from his as she glanced back at the storeroom. "And what are my father and Gianna doing?"

"Your father is holding down the fort, and Gianna sent me out to ask if you'll talk with her privately."

Cat frowned. "Of course, I will. Why would she have to ask?"

"I think she's embarrassed that she caused this whole situation by trying to placate her mother with the story that you were seeing someone. She's afraid you'll hate her now."

"Of course, I don't hate her. I'd actually forgotten that it was her storytelling that started this whole fake engagement thing."

He suppressed the urge to reach for her hand again. But he couldn't prevent himself from saying, "When this is over, we'll talk."

This time when the nerves flashed into her eyes, he felt some satisfaction since they echoed the ones jittering in his stomach. Around them chaos reigned as people jostled their way to displays or to the checkout counter. A child laughed, an adult scolded, and above it all, "I'll be Home for Christmas" filled the air. There was a part of him that wanted to settle things between them, but it was the wrong time, and certainly the wrong place.

Instead, he drew her into his arms, and after a second's hesitation, she laid her head on his shoulder. Just for a moment. "You're doing fine. Your uncle Jack has updated your father on everything that's happened."

"Shit," breathed Cat into his shirt.

"I figure that at the ball the colonel will provide one more set of eyes watching you."

She drew back then and met his eyes. "You're worried."

"No," he lied. All morning long, he'd been telling himself that there was no reason to be worried. But it was there, a steady thrum in the blood.

"I had Jase check out your office earlier, and he's up there now making sure it's empty. Once he comes down, it will be safe for you and Gianna to talk there. Jase will make sure no one disturbs you."

Drawing back, Cat nodded and made herself step away. As Dino headed toward the storeroom, his words drifted into her mind again. *When this is over, we'll talk.*

Why did that make her more nervous than the charade she was going to act out at the ball tonight?

The jangling of the bell over the shop door had Cat whirling toward it. This time it was Orlando, the Merceri family chauffeur who entered. Cat saw an instant of hesitation as he glanced around the crowded store. But he recovered smoothly once he spotted her and headed in her direction.

"Signora McGuire called me on my cell and asked me to bring this in for you." Orlando offered her the dress bag he was carrying.

Cat recognized the designer name discreetly printed on the top and took it from Orlando just as Gianna reached her.

"It's a peace offering," her stepmother said. "I want to talk to you."

Cat led the way up the spiral staircase, noting when she reached the top that Jase sat down on the first step as soon as Gianna moved past him, effectively blocking anyone from following them. To anyone who glanced his way, Dino's friend appeared to be playing with a puzzle game.

Gianna wasted no time once they were in Cat's office. "I'm so sorry."

"For what?" Cat hung the dress bag carefully on a hook.

"For getting you into this." Gianna threw her hands up and began to pace. "I don't expect you to understand. From what Jimmy says your mother was perfect."

"She was a special woman." Cat studied her stepmother. Gianna Merceri McGuire was the most pulled-together and composed woman she'd ever met. Cat hardly recognized the woman who was nervously pacing in front of her.

"I've lived all my life trying to measure up to my mother's expectations. She chose my first husband, and I went along with it." Gianna waved a hand. "Don't get me wrong. Donatello was a nice man, and he was very good at running the New York branch of Merceri Bank. I wasn't unhappy with him, and he gave me my daughter, Lucy. And I became exactly what my mother wanted me to become—a New York society matron."

She glanced at Cat, lifted her chin. "And I'm not unhappy with that, either." Gianna ran her fingers through her hair. "I'm rambling."

"What do you want to tell me, Gianna?" Cat asked softly.

"I was wrong to tell my mother you were seeing someone, and that I was pretty certain you'd be announcing your engagement in the near future. I've spent my whole life doing what my mother wanted. She told me she wanted great-grand-children, and I nudged Lucy to produce one. But you were… different. I couldn't nudge you in the direction my mother wanted. So I took the coward's way out and lied. Each time I told the story, I embroidered it a bit more. That was wrong. I should have stood up to her and defended you."

Gianna threw up her hands again. "Why should you have become the perfect model of a Merceri woman just because I married your father?"

When she paused as if waiting for an answer, Cat moved forward and took her hands. "I guess we can agree on that one."

Gianna squeezed her fingers. "I'm so angry with myself."

"Don't be."

"This whole mess started me thinking. What if my mother had objected to my marrying your father? I can't help wondering if I would have just gone meekly along with her decision." Keeping her gaze steady on Cat's, Gianna said, "That would have been a huge mistake because I love your father so much. I can't bear to think that I might have lost him."

Seeing the tears swim in Gianna's eyes, Cat threw her arms around her stepmother. "My father wouldn't have given up. He wouldn't have let you walk away."

Gianna drew back. "You think not?"

"I know not. He has a way of getting what he wants. And he's just as involved in this fake engagement charade as you are."

Gianna shrugged. "He just did it to save my neck."

"No. I mean it probably started out as a plan to save your neck, but then I think the plot expanded. He didn't just hire anyone off the street to play the role."

As she thought more about it, Cat began to pace. "He consulted with my godfather, Admiral Maxwell, and they hand-picked Navy Captain Dino Angelis."

Whirling, she fisted her hands on her hips and faced

Gianna. "I think he and Uncle Bobby decided to do a little matchmaking of their own."

Something flared in Gianna's eyes. "So Jimmy's not just trying to rescue me?"

"Not by a long shot." She couldn't tell Gianna about the more complex part of the masquerade. The fewer people who knew about the drug smuggling, the better. But she could certainly share the part she was just figuring out herself.

"I think he wants to see me married off as much as you and your mother do." Cat's eyes narrowed. "I wouldn't put it past him to have called your mother and planted the whole surprise Christmas visit in her head."

"Really." Gianna began to tap her foot. Then she threw her hands up in the air again. "The thing is, I think he's right."

"About what?"

"About you and Dino Angelis. I like your navy captain. Did you hear the way he defended you to my mother? No one stands up to her that way. And she liked it. She likes him, too. That was the other thing I wanted to talk to you about. Even if you're right about your father, I think you ought to grab the guy."

Knots twisted in Cat's stomach. "It's not that simple. He's from San Francisco, and his family is important to him. I run a store in New York."

Gianna smiled slowly. "So you have thought about it."

Cat was pretty sure she'd been thinking about it from the first time he'd strolled into the store and kissed her. "I think I love him."

Once the words were out, the knots in her stomach grew even tighter. "But I don't think he feels the same way. Once the ball is over, he says we're going to talk. I'm pretty sure he's going to tell me why he has to leave." Cat paused, took a deep breath. "I don't know why I'm unloading all this on you."

"You're talking to me because I'm another woman. If I hadn't been so influenced by my mother's agenda, we might have grown closer before this. I'm sorry about that, too. But the most important thing is what you're going to do when you and Dino Angelis talk."

This time Cat felt her stomach take a tumble. "He's a very kind man. He's going to let me down easily."

"And then you'll tell him what you want. And you're going to go after it." Gianna smiled at her. Cat realized that it was the first genuine smile Gianna had ever given her. "Didn't you just tell me that your father never would have let me walk away?"

Cat nodded.

"Well, you're your father's daughter. And you'll get your captain." She motioned to the dress bag. "I brought this as a peace offering, but I think it will work nicely on your Dino."

13

WITH DINO'S HAND at the small of her back, Cat dashed to the open door of the limo, ducked in and slid to the far end of the cushy leather seat. Outside, Dino paused to pass their duffels and her dress bag to the uniformed driver. She took the opportunity to close her eyes and summon up a kaleidoscope of images—the faces of her employees when she'd announced she was leaving early for the charity ball and that she was taking the doll with her.

She felt Dino slide in beside her, heard the door slam shut while in her mind's eye, she recalled expressions of surprise on Matt's and Josie's faces. But she was almost sure it was delight and approval she'd seen on Adelaide's. On her way to the door, her assistant manager had placed a hand on her arm and murmured in a voice only Cat could hear, "Good for you. If I had a hot-looking fiancé, I'd have knocked off at noon."

She'd smiled at Adelaide, but she wondered now if the woman she'd thought of as a close friend was only playing a role—and a deadly one at that. As the limo eased away from the curb, Cat let out a frustrated sigh and began to run the day's events through her mind again. But there was nothing there—nothing in anything her employees had said or done that was definitively suspicious.

She fisted her hands on the leather seat. "I'm absolutely

no good at playing detective. I've been watching them like a hawk all day. But I'm still clueless about whether it's Matt, Josie or Adelaide who's unloading the drugs on this end."

"We need a break," Dino said.

"But what if we don't get one? What if this whole trap we're setting turns out to be a bust?"

"I'm not talking about a break in the case."

The sound of a cork popping had her opening her eyes. Dino tipped wine into two flutes and Cat watched bubbles fizz to the rim. Then he handed her a glass and raised his in a toast.

"To breaks."

There was something in his eyes that had her blood heating, her heart pumping. She sipped her champagne. "What kind of break are you thinking of— exactly?"

Dino took the glass from her and set it with his on a small tray. "I suggested to the driver that he take a circuitous route to the Alsatian Towers—to make sure we weren't being followed."

Cat glanced back over her shoulder through the smoky glass. Though it was only four, cars had their headlights on. And traffic was heavy. "Do you think someone is on our tail?"

"No. There's no need. Everyone knows where we're going."

"Then why— -" When she turned back, he'd moved close enough to trace a finger down her throat to where her sweater formed a V. The tremor skittered through her all the way to the pit of her stomach.

"Twelve hours," he murmured. "Twelve endless hours. That's how long I've been wanting to touch you and couldn't."

He framed her face with his hands and Cat felt the pressure of each one of his fingers. But it was the heat in his eyes that transfixed her.

"I shouldn't be touching you. I told myself I wouldn't until this is over. But I couldn't stop myself from making love to you last night. And I can't help myself right now."

The thread of frustration she heard in his voice had a feeling of power moving through her. "Go ahead. Touch me. I want you to."

He drew her closer, brushed his mouth over hers. His tongue slipped between her lips and slid over hers. Then he traced a line of featherlight kisses to her ear and whispered, "Have you ever made love in a limo before?"

Heat arrowed through her. "No."

"We'll have to be fast and quiet."

He was already moving quickly, shifting to the floor so that he was between her knees and pulling her slacks off. She heard his breath catch and then his fingers began to toy with the lace at the top of her thigh-high stockings. Pleasure spiked through her as he traced a lazy pattern higher and higher on her legs.

"Fast," she reminded him.

"Oh, I think we have a little time." Pushing aside the thin lace of her panties, he slipped two fingers into her.

She arched. *"Dino."*

"Shh." He crushed her mouth with his.

It was her turn to move quickly then as she dragged off his belt and ripped open the snap on his jeans. It took both of them to get the jeans down his hips. Then he made quick work of the condom, tearing off the foil and slipping it on. She helped him by pulling aside her panties.

And then she bit down hard on her lip as she watched him push slowly into her body. Pressure and heat shot through her. Dizzy with the sensation of his penetration, Cat met his eyes and what she saw in them—the desperation, the longing—was enough to trigger the first convulsion. As it rippled through

her in an ever-widening wave of pleasure, she wrapped arms
and legs around him.

Dino waited, keeping his own needs reined in. Her eyes
were open and on his, and he knew as her climax peaked that
she thought only of him.

Then he began to move, one stroke and then another. On
his third thrust, she began to move with him, settling into his
rhythm. He'd planned to keep his movements slow, to draw
out the pleasure for both of them, but as she tightened around
him again, he felt his control begin to shred. In the dim, inter-
mittent flash of streetlights, all he could see was her. First in
shadow, then in light. The effect was incredibly erotic.

As his need built, all he could think of was Cat. All he
wanted was Cat. Grasping her hips, he pushed into her faster
and harder until all he knew was Cat. She filled him until there
was nothing else, no one else but the long explosion of
pleasure that they brought each other.

Afterward, he held her tightly against him, for his own sake
as much as hers. He didn't want to let her go. Couldn't let her
go. And he was going to have to tell her. Soon.

DINO HAD TO HAND IT to Gianna Merceri McGuire. She'd trans-
formed the Grand Ballroom of the Alsatian Towers into a
Christmas fantasy. Twinkling white lights cascaded from the
ceiling, competing with the glow of the crystal chandeliers.
White poinsettia plants lined three mirrored walls and were
clustered at intervals along the dance floor. The scent of candles
blended with expensive perfume. Silver gleamed on snow-
white tablecloths, and a wall of French doors opened onto a
glassed-in terrace offering a view of the Manhattan skyline.

For over an hour, Cat had stood next to her very pregnant
stepsister at the end of the reception line, greeting guests as

hey'd filed in to fill their assigned tables. No one could tell by looking at her animated expression the kind of day she'd put in.

Nor what she still had to do.

The woman was amazing. Before they'd left the shop, she'd plucked the damaged doll out of the display window and everyone had seen her tuck it into a Cheshire Cat gift bag.

Right now that gift bag was in plain sight at the McGuires' reserved table, and the hair of the doll was just visible. Jack Phillips, who had gone through the reception line early on, was now seated within arm's reach of the "bait," entertaining Lucia Merceri until her family joined her. Across from him sat Admiral Robert Maxwell and his wife who'd also been among the first to arrive.

His admiral's presence had come as a surprise to Dino. And it worried him a bit. He didn't doubt for a moment that Cat's father had filled his best friend in on exactly the kind of trap they were setting tonight.

The problem was the ballroom now contained a lot of people who were concerned for Cat's safety and who wanted to nail the bastard who was behind the drug smuggling. Hopefully when something went down, they wouldn't all trip over each other. An even bigger problem was that even though he'd watched every person who'd made their way through the line, he hadn't gotten any "feelings" about any of them. In fact, the only thing his gut instinct had been telling him since he'd entered the ballroom was that Cat was in danger.

Dino shifted his gaze back to Jack. From the look on Phillips' face, he wasn't having an easy time of it with Lucia. But in Dino's opinion, the woman wasn't nearly the ogre that everyone made her out to be. His mother had enjoyed her conversation with Lucia immensely.

Dino let his gaze sweep the room which was nearly full

now. When they'd arrived, Matt Winslow, Josie Sullivan and Adelaide Creed had been escorted to a table near the back of the ballroom. He'd noted Dr. and Mrs. Lassiter's entrance with interest. They'd been seated closer to the dance floor in what looked to be an area reserved for VIPs. Dino recognized some of the other people at the Lassiters' table—the governor, a state senator, a film star. But it was the woman seated between the governor and Mrs. Lassiter who drew his gaze. She was striking in a long-sleeved black sequined dress. Bangs fringed her forehead and the rest of her dark hair fell in a smooth line to her shoulders.

When Dino sensed Jase at his side, he said, "Who's the woman in the black dress sitting next to the governor?"

"Jessica Atwell, our famous 'get kids off drugs' attorney general. If you were a New Yorker, you'd recognize her from the TV campaign she's been running. She's even got her face on a billboard over Times Square."

Dino was about to look away when Jessica Atwell took out a pair of reading glasses and put them on. A tingle of awareness moved through him—the first he'd had all evening. "What else do you know about her?"

"Just what everyone knows. She started out forty years ago in Hollywood and made several movies. Then she became an activist and later a congresswoman. Word is she's trying to raise money for a Senate run."

Dino glanced back to the McGuires' table. Jack was standing.

"You'd better get back in position," Dino said. "It looks like Jack Phillips is headed toward the bar."

Jase was seated at the table next to the McGuires'. If anyone made a grab for the doll, he and Jack were in charge of grabbing the person. But Dino's gut feeling was that it wasn't going to go down that easily. What he didn't like, didn't like

t all was his lingering feeling that in spite of the precautions
ne and Jack and Colonel McGuire had taken, Cat was in
mortal danger.

It was the same feeling that had thrummed through his
blood before he'd taken a bullet on his last op. Not good.

His gaze returned to Cat. Another problem all evening had
been taking his eyes off of her. Ever since she'd changed into
that dress her stepmother had brought as a peace offering,
she'd simply stolen his breath away. The red silk clung to her
like a second skin, and the view from the back was even more
dangerous to his breathing than the view from the front. In his
opinion, the dress perfectly captured the passion of the woman.

But even without the dress, she was beautiful. He'd known
that from the first time he'd looked at her photo. But now he
knew the depth of that beauty. She was smart and strong and
passionate. And she'd done a hell of a job that day at the store.

While she'd been watching her employees, he'd been
watching her, and she'd done nothing, said nothing to indicate
to any one of them that she knew anything about the drugs
that had been smuggled into the country through her store. If
he'd still been in the business of undercover ops, he'd want
her on his team.

"She's a beautiful woman."

"Yes." Dino swore silently as he turned to face Matt
Winslow. He hadn't sensed the man's approach. His mind had
been too filled with Cat.

Matt carried two glasses of champagne and he sipped one
of them as he studied Dino. Winslow had been animated and
smiling in the reception line, but now his eyes were assess-
ing, his expression cool.

"How did you and Cat meet?"

The blunt question had Dino wondering if the man was a

suspicious drug mule—or just jealous. As far as he knew, Cat looked on Matt Winslow as a brother. Had Matt wanted a deeper relationship? Or was he merely being protective of a friend? "Cat didn't tell you?"

"She's never even mentioned you," Matt said. "I was under the impression that since she opened the store, she wasn't dating, didn't have the time. And we hardly had the chance to chat today in the store."

He *had* wanted more, Dino decided. And he'd thought he'd have plenty of time to make his move. Dino might have worked up some sympathy for Winslow, if he hadn't wondered exactly how a man found the control to bide his time with a woman like Cat McGuire. He hadn't even been able to wait until his bodyguarding job was over.

And just why had Winslow been so willing to wait? He recalled what Cat had told him—that Matt saw the Cheshire Cat as a stepping-stone and that his goal was to become a millionaire. Was smuggling drugs another stepping-stone?

"Well?" Impatience shimmered in Matt's tone.

"We ran into each other a couple of months ago on the skating rink at Rockefeller Center. Literally. A week ago, I proposed to her there."

Matt frowned. "She never told me she'd started skating again. I would have gone with her."

Dino met his eyes levelly. "Evidently, there are lots of things she doesn't tell you." Beyond Matt's shoulder, Dino spotted Jack at a nearby drink station.

"Excuse me." He moved past Matt to join Jack at the bar.

"You're supposed to be guarding Cat's bag."

"I'm on a mission to get her royal highness a martini, straight up with an olive. An Italian olive. Working undercover for the CIA is a lot easier than this."

Dino grinned.

"If anyone goes for the doll while I'm gone, Signora Merceri will take them out with her cane."

Dino didn't doubt it for a moment. "You should know that I'm beginning to get a bad feeling about this."

Frowning, Jack took the martini from the waiter behind the bar. "We've got everything covered."

"Just wanted to let you know."

Jack had no sooner drifted away in the direction of the McGuires' table when the reception line broke up, and Cat turned to join him. Together they fell in line behind Gianna and her father. As they moved to their table, waiters flowed into the room and began to serve the first course.

"The ball has officially begun," Cat murmured.

Dino let his gaze sweep the room, tracking the usual suspects. This time, for a long moment, his gaze locked with someone else's. A heightening of awareness, a surge of adrenaline, mixed with surprise. He strongly suspected he was looking into the eyes of the person who was running the drug smuggling operation. It was only a premonition, a "hunch." But if he was right, it more than explained the attempt on Cat's life.

He had no way of proving it. Not yet. But his mind raced as he pulled out Cat's chair and settled himself in the one next to hers. Others had to be involved, and one of them would provide the link.

The question was who would make the move on Cat to get that doll?

IT WAS NEARLY AN HOUR before the dancing began. Gianna and her father were the first to rise from their table. Her stepsister Lucy and her husband followed, then Dino offered his hand. Cat put hers into it, rose and moved with him to the dance floor.

The moment she stepped into his arms, she felt his tension. "You're worried."

"Just watchful."

"Nothing's happening." Impatience rolled through her. "Maybe we were wrong to think that someone would make a move tonight. Maybe they're not even here."

"They're here all right. I think I know who's behind the drug operation."

She met his eyes and saw the truth of his statement. "Who?"

Instead of answering immediately, he danced her across the floor. "Look at the people seated at the table directly to your right."

Cat glanced at the table. "Mrs. Lassiter?"

"No. Look again."

This time she let her gaze sweep the table more slowly. She recognized a state senator, the governor, the attorney general, and a film star whose name she couldn't quite pull up. Then as if they could feel her gaze, one of them looked up and met her eyes. And suddenly the memory that had been tugging at the edge of her mind for a day and a half clicked. "It's George Miller."

"I think so, too," Dino murmured as he swung her to the center of the dance floor. "But there's no evidence we can take to anyone yet."

"What are we going to do?"

"There has to be an accomplice—one of your employees. So we'll go ahead with our plan and hope that they can provide the proof we need."

Her uncle Bobby tapped Dino on the shoulder. "My turn."

Her godfather smiled down at her when Cat stepped into his arms, but his eyes were serious. "Are you all right?"

"Don't I look all right?"

"A little tense, that's all. But you still manage to look beautiful."

"You're biased."

Her godfather laughed then, and for a moment Cat felt almost normal—as if she were just a woman dancing with her father's best friend at a Christmas ball. As he swirled her toward the center of the dance floor, she relaxed in his arms.

"So what do you think of Dino Angelis?"

Cat's eyes shifted to where Dino was standing at the edge of the dance floor. He was wearing his navy dress uniform and just the sight of him had her pulse leaping. Then Cat narrowed her gaze on her godfather. The innocent look in his eyes had her recalling her earlier conversation with Gianna and it confirmed her suspicions.

"What do I think of him? What I think is that when you and my dad selected Captain Dino Angelis to be my bodyguard, a certain amount of meddling matchmaking was involved."

"Meddling?" Maxwell frowned. "I don't know what you're talking about. Your father called me, told me what he suspected was going on at your store, and I sent my best man."

Cat stepped back out of his arms and tapped a finger on his chest. "You can just cut the innocent act. I've already told Gianna what I think went down. I'll bet you and my father even have a little wager riding on the outcome."

Maxwell's face remained blank. "I'm taking the Fifth."

She snorted. "How much did you bet?"

"You're too smart for your own good."

Cat fisted her hands on her hips. "How much?"

The admiral sighed. "All right. I bet him fifty bucks that you and Angelis would hit it off and that the engagement would become real."

A little band tightened around Cat's heart. "Well, it's not

going to become real." She might want it to—in spite of the fact that she'd been set up—but…

"Dino's family lives in San Francisco. One of his cousins is getting married two days after Christmas. Once he's finished his job with me, he's going to be on the first plane out of here."

Unless she followed her stepmother's advice and persuaded him differently. Or went with him?

FROM THE SIDE of the dance floor, Dino watched as Cat and his admiral danced. The ballroom was growing warmer, and behind him, wait staff were opening the French doors to the terrace.

Suddenly, Cat and the admiral stopped dancing. She poked a finger into his chest.

Dino took one step forward, intending to cut in for another dance and rescue his boss when a vision slammed into him, filling his mind. Someone pointing a gun at Cat.

Fear froze him to the spot.

On the rare occasions when he experienced them, his visions were only a blurry flash—a quickly fading image in black and white. Cat was in a confined space—an elevator? A closet? The details weren't clear. And it was too dark to make out the face of the person holding the gun on her. He couldn't even be sure if it was a man or a woman.

Then all he saw was a flash of fire as the bullet exploded from the gun.

For a moment, his heart simply stopped. Someone was going to get to Cat and he couldn't tell who it was.

Or how to stop it.

14

"YOU OKAY?"

The voice was barely audible, but Dino recognized that it belonged to Jase who was standing to his right. He pulled himself together. Dancers swirled past them, and Dino finally spotted Cat now dancing with her father.

Without looking at Jase or acknowledging his presence in any way, Dino spoke in a voice that didn't carry. "Someone's going to get to her and they have a gun." Fear had formed a tight knot in his stomach.

"Got any details?"

Keeping his gaze locked on Cat, Dino filled Jase in on what he'd seen and what he knew.

"Have you told her?" Jase asked.

"About the person I suspect is running the operation—yes. She agrees. Something about Mr. George Miller struck her as familiar the moment he stepped into her shop. But I haven't told her that someone is going to hold her at gunpoint."

"I'd do it now," Jase said.

Moving to the dance floor, Dino tapped Colonel McGuire on the shoulder and once more took Cat into his arms. Then he skillfully steered her through the open French doors to the terrace.

THE DIMLY LIT SERVICE HALLWAY that led from the ballroom to the kitchen was deserted except for the two figures. Scents from the recently served dinner mingled with the smell of cleanser. The sound of the orchestra and the chatter of the guests were muted here.

One of the figures was partially hidden behind an open door. "You've studied the blueprint I gave you?"

"Yes."

"Here's the syringe, the key and the gun."

All three were slipped into a pocket. "She's being very well guarded. Her uncle is here—he's CIA. And her fiancé never lets her get more than a few feet away."

"Do I have to spell out everything? There's one place she can go where the men can't follow her."

There was silence as a waiter hurried by carrying a tray of dirty china and silver to the kitchen.

"Remember that when you've got the doll, Ms. McGuire must be eliminated."

Fear turned icy, and the words gushed out. "I didn't sign on for murder. I don't know if I—"

"You can and you will." The voice was calm, cold. "If she hasn't already figured out that you betrayed her, she will soon. Think of it this way. It's Ms. McGuire or you. If I have to take steps, I'll eliminate you, too."

The figure half hidden behind the door stepped out and walked back into the ballroom.

"THIS IS BETTER," Dino murmured as he guided her toward the railing that lined the glass-walled terrace. Beyond it, the skyline of Manhattan shone as brightly as any Christmas tree. "I need to talk to you for a moment."

Cat turned to him. "I need to talk to you, too. I found out that this whole fake fiancé thing is a setup."

Dino studied her. "We both knew that it was a cover so that I could protect you."

Cat waved a hand. "I'm not talking about that. I'm talking about the fact that my father and Uncle Bobby have a second hidden agenda here. They're playing matchmakers and hoping that the engagement will take, that it will become real."

She whirled to pace a few feet away. "In fact, your boss has even bet fifty bucks on a successful outcome."

She paused, waiting for a reaction. When Dino said nothing, she strode toward him. "You're not surprised? Were you in on it?"

Dino raised both hands, palms out. "No way."

Cat put her hands on her hips. "How did you figure it out?" She narrowed her eyes. "Was it some kind of precognition? Because if it was, you should have—"

"It wasn't."

"When did you know?"

"I'm not sure, but I got an inkling that the setup was a bit more complicated than your father was letting on when I first met him in his office."

Cat began to tap her foot. "What did he say? He and I are going to have a little talk about this."

Dino moved toward her and placed his hands on her shoulders. "It wasn't anything definitive. Just as I was leaving the office, he mentioned that while I was pulling off the charade and bodyguarding you without your catching on, he'd appreciate it if I saw to it that you had some fun. And usually fathers don't ask soldiers to show their daughters a good time."

"I'm going to kill him," Cat said. "Better still, I'm going

to steal his secret cache of cigars and destroy them." She met his eyes. "I'm sorry."

He kissed her forehead. "I'm the one who should apologize. I really haven't gotten around to making sure you're having fun."

She smiled then. "Not true. I'd say that what we did in the limo was the most fun I've had in a long time—unless you count the fun we had in my office—or on the floor of my apartment—or—"

Dino silenced her then by pulling her close for a kiss. It had temper, nerves and fear streaming away. When he finally released her, she was breathless and tingling.

"I needed that," Dino said.

"Me, too."

"We'll have more fun, I promise, but I brought you out here to tell you something."

"What?"

He told her about the vision.

She met his eyes steadily. "I think it's a sign."

"It's a sign all right, and I don't like it. I didn't see enough."

"I think you did. If we want this person to make his or her move, we have to give them the opportunity. And we discussed the best scenario for that. You ask Gianna to dance and I take the doll and head to the washroom. If Matt's involved, he'll make his move then. If it's Josie or Adelaide, they'll follow me into the ladies' room."

"Jasc's operative is stationed there. She's dressed as a washroom attendant, and she's supposed to make a move if someone follows you. But it's not going to go down the way we want it to."

"Because of your vision, we know that. So we've been forewarned."

Dino grasped her shoulders again. "I still don't like it."

"Neither do I. But it's a chance we have to take if we're going to catch the people behind this and put them away."

Dino pulled her close, held her tight. "Just remember that Jase and I won't be far behind."

"Don't worry. I'm not about to forget that." Cat allowed herself to stay in his arms for just another moment before she led the way back into the ballroom.

THE MOMENT CAT STEPPED into the hall outside the ballroom, she saw Matt standing across the way, as if he'd been waiting. She ruthlessly pushed away fear, disappointment and anger as he strode toward her, and summoned up a smile. Matt didn't return it. All she read was anger and something else in his eyes. Hurt?

"Can we talk for a moment? In private?" Without waiting for her assent, he took her arm in a firm grip and steered her to the end of the corridor. When they reached it, Cat saw that hallways branched off to the left and to the right. If Matt pulled her into one of them…

She didn't dare look behind her to see if either Jase or Dino had stepped out of the ballroom yet. Instead, she dug in her heels. "This is private enough. What is it, Matt?"

"Your engagement. Why didn't you tell me about it?"

She studied him, trying to read his expression. He hadn't released his grip on her arm. "I didn't tell anyone."

"Well, you should have. You told me you weren't dating. You didn't have time for relationships. I respected that. And I waited. I was trying to give you the time and the space you needed before I told you how I felt. And now…"

He wasn't the one who'd betrayed her, Cat thought as twin waves of relief and sympathy moved through her. "I never lied to you. I wasn't dating until I met Dino. And I wasn't looking for a relationship until him."

Matt turned, paced away, then turned back to face her. "I should have spoken sooner. Would it have made a difference if I had?"

Cat shook her head. "What I feel for you, what I've always felt for you is friendship."

Though he didn't move a muscle, Cat could see that her words struck him hard.

"Friendship." There was bitterness in his tone. "There's no way I can change your mind?"

Cat thought of Dino, and if she hadn't known it before, she did then—he was the only man in the world for her. "No. But I hope we can continue being friends, Matt."

He didn't say anything. Cat watched in sadness as he turned and made his way back into the ballroom. She saw no sign of either Jase or Dino. But then she wasn't supposed to. The whole idea was that she was to appear alone, vulnerable. Taking a deep breath, she walked back down the hallway toward the ladies' room.

She'd told everyone at the table that she was going to the restroom. Whoever was watching had to have seen her pick up the gift bag and leave.

Right now she could feel goose bumps on her arms and hairs on the back of her neck were standing up. Someone was watching her. She was sure of it. She suppressed the urge to whirl around and see who it was. Instead, she reached for the door handle and entered the ladies' room.

Lounge was a more appropriate word, Cat decided as she took in the French Impressionist prints, the leather cushioned seats and the mirrored wall. One woman in what Cat was sure was a Dior design was retouching her lipstick. There was no sign of a washroom attendant.

The woman met Cat's eyes in the mirror and said, "You're Gianna's stepdaughter, right?"

"Yes."

Rising, the woman extended her hand. "Lydia Hathaway. I worked on one of her committees for this extravaganza. She speaks highly of you."

Cat shook the hand. "Nice meeting you."

When the woman walked out, Cat moved into a second room lined on one side with closed stall doors and on the other side with marble sinks. Two of them were in use. One of the ladies was gray-haired with a queen's ransom of diamonds dangling from her ears. The other one was in her midtwenties and looked as if she was battling an eating disorder. The older woman left first, and two other women entered from the lounge area and stepped into stalls.

Where was Jase's operative? Cat's nerves tightened as she moved to a sink and turned on one of the faucets. Then her stomach sank as she glanced in the mirror and saw a very familiar figure step out of the first stall and move toward her. She managed a smile before she dropped her eyes and tried to gather her thoughts.

Play dumb. Stall her.

"Cat, I was hoping for an opportunity to talk with you. Your stepmother has outdone herself this year."

"Gianna excels at this sort of thing."

As another woman stepped out of the stall and moved to a sink, Cat felt something hard press into her side. The voice in her ear was barely a whisper. "The washroom attendant is unconscious in the stall I just left. If you don't want someone else to get hurt, you're going to lead the way to that door over there."

"I don't understand." Cat spoke softly as she moved to door marked Storage. "What's going on?"

"We're taking a little walk." Reaching around Cat she shoved a key in the door and opened it.

Disbelief, disappointment, fear. Cat struggled to suppress the emotions flooding through her as she led the way into a small room. She had time to note the large cart filled with cleaning supplies before the door swung shut, cutting off all the light.

Was this what Dino had seen in his vision?

Panic rose, but Cat fought it back. She needed a clear head. A shot would be too risky here. Still, Cat jumped when the gun poked into her back.

"Move. The exit door is just ahead of you."

Stretching her hands out in front of her, Cat groped for the handle, turned it, and stepped into an empty corridor. Doors on either side led to hotel staff offices, all closed for the night. The music from the ballroom was faint. Cat realized that the chance of party guests wandering this far was slim to none. How was Dino going to find her?

At gunpoint, Cat led the way across the hall, through a door, and into a stairwell. A lightbulb overhead barely illuminated the steep flight of stairs and the narrow landing below.

A sinking feeling in her stomach told her this was the place Dino had seen in his vision. Panic surged again, and Cat forced herself to take deep calming breaths.

"We're going down. We're still too close to the ballroom. I don't want to make it easy for your protectors to find you."

"My protectors?"

"Don't play dumb. Your fiancé, your uncle, your father— and I'm sure there are more. It wasn't hard to spot the woman they had staked out in the ladies' room." The gun poked her again. "Move. I won't hesitate to use this."

tall. Stall. As she reached the landing at the bottom of
the first flight of stairs, Cat made herself stumble and fall
to her knees.

"No, you don't. Get up or I'll shoot you here."

Cat got to her feet and they descended two more flights.

"Far enough. Put the bag on the floor and then back up a
couple of steps."

Facing the barrel of the gun, Cat's mind raced as fast as
her heart. She thought of the woman she'd known for a year
and a half. The woman she'd worked with, laughed with. It
couldn't have all been an act.

"You don't want to do this. Even if you get away with the
doll, you're going to be discovered and arrested. The FBI,
the CIA—they're all looking at the store. They're closing in."

"You're lying. Put down the doll." Her voice was firm, but
the hand holding the gun trembled until she brought her other
hand up to steady it.

Cat drew the bag around in front of her, using it as a shield.
If she pulled the trigger, she'd have to risk putting a bullet
through the drugs. "Why, Adelaide? Don't I at least deserve
an answer to that?"

SOMETHING WAS WRONG. The bad feeling he'd had all day so-
lidified in Dino's gut. Three full minutes had dragged by, and
there'd been a steady stream of women entering and leaving
the ladies' room. Not one of them had carried anything large
enough to hold the doll.

And Cat hadn't returned.

As he strode to the door, Jase joined him. "Winslow's at
the bar. Josie's still at the table, but Adelaide and our prime
suspect are missing."

"Adelaide didn't follow Cat into the washroom."

"Maybe she was already in there."

Dino's hand was on the knob when a vision flashed into his mind. He could only see their backs, but he recognized Cat and the woman holding a gun on her—Adelaide. Cat led the way though a door with an Exit sign over it. The image was fading to gray, but before it vanished, Dino made out the letters on the door—*Stairs*.

The vision had barely faded before another filled his mind. The same one he'd seen before—Cat and a person holding a gun in a dimly lit space. Once again he saw the flash of fire and heard the deafening sound of a gunshot.

Pushing down his fear, Dino whirled away from the ladies' room and strode back to where one of the hotel employees was standing at the entrance to the ballroom. To forestall questions, he said, "This may be an emergency. Where are the staircases on this floor?"

"There are two—"

"Which one is closer?"

The young man pointed to the end of the corridor. "Take a left. Should I notify someone?" he asked.

Dino was already running. "We'll let you know."

With Jase at his side, Dino went left and prayed that he'd made the right choice. When they reached the stairs, he gripped the handle, turned the knob carefully and pushed the door open just a crack. He heard voices. Signaling Jase to stay where he was and hold the door ajar, Dino slipped through a narrow opening and moved quietly to the railing. On a landing, three flights down, he saw Cat clutching the gift bag to her chest. He couldn't see Adelaide's face, but he saw the hands holding the gun. They were shaking.

Then he caught it. Just the barest hint of a shadow on a lower level, slowly climbing toward Cat and Adelaide.

Fear pounded through him. Backing up, he whispered to Jase what to do and quietly closed the stairwell door. Then he slipped out of his shoes and silently started down the stairs.

15

"Why did I do it?" Adelaide's mouth twisted slightly. "Money, of course."

Cat's eyes widened. "You can't need it. I know that you're not earning a lot in my shop, but you have your retirement money."

"*Had* my retirement money. A year ago, I got greedy and took some risks with my investments. When they didn't pay off, I took more risks. I came to work for you because I needed the money. And that's when she approached me."

"Who?" In spite of the dim lighting, Cat could read fear in the other woman's eyes. "You're talking about Jessica Atwell, aren't you?"

Adelaide's face drained of color and her voice dropped to a whisper. "How do you know?"

"She's on TV all the time. The moment that George Miller walked into the shop, I knew there was something familiar about him. At first I thought he reminded me of Santa Claus. But he has Jessica Atwell's eyes. What exactly did she ask you to do?"

"She'd done her research—on both of us. She knew your family connections and that your reputation was stellar. She also knew I was desperate for money. And she offered me a lot. All I had to do was to make sure certain toys that you imported from Paxco got to her. It was so easy."

Above the sound of Adelaide's voice, Cat thought she heard the sound of a door opening somewhere below them. Was it wishful thinking? Or was it Dino? She badly wanted to shift her gaze to the railing and glance down, but she kept her eyes on Adelaide.

"Who handled the Paxco end?" Cat asked. "Was it Matt?"

"No. I don't know what went on in Mexico. Just before a shipment, I would get a phone call describing the toy the drugs were in."

AT THE NEXT LANDING, Dino edged as close as he dared to the railing and glanced down. The shadow he'd seen earlier was clearer now. Light glinted off the sequins on the dress the woman was wearing. There wasn't a doubt in his mind that it was Jessica Atwell and she was closer to Cat and Adelaide than he was.

No sign of Jase. But there wouldn't be. Fading back to the wall, Dino increased his pace. He heard women's voices more clearly, but he still couldn't make out what they were saying.

Keep her talking, Cat. I'm almost there.

Two landings above Cat and Adelaide, he paused. Once he started down the next flight of stairs, Adelaide would be able to see him if she glanced up, and she still had her gun aimed at Cat. Dino waited, biding his time.

"ONCE I KNEW which one carried the drugs, I'd write up the order in a fake name, pay for it with cash, and that night, a limousine would be waiting a few blocks away. I'd deliver the package on my way to the subway. Six months, she promised, and I'd make back twice what I'd lost. I did. Then she kept saying one more shipment. She had customers she couldn't disappoint. It's been a year. But this is the end of it. Once you're gone, the operation will be over. I'll be free. Give me the damn doll."

Cat backed up a step and clutched the bag more cl[...] "Giving her the doll won't end this for you. She's goin[...] have to kill you."

"No." Adelaide nearly shouted the word. "She told me [...] was you or me. It's going to be you. Give me the bag."

"She can't afford to let you live." In her peripheral vision, Cat could see a shadow on the stairs below them. Praying that it was Dino or Jase, she kept her gaze steady on Adelaide. She had to keep the woman's attention focused on her so she backed up onto the first step of the stairs they'd just descended.

"She has two sets of customers. Did you know that?"

Adelaide took a step toward her. "What are you talking about?"

"There's the people she supplies with the drugs, and then there's the terrorist cell she funds with the profits."

Adelaide's eyes widened. "You're lying."

"You didn't know?"

"No. I would never— No."

"That will work in your favor. If you name her, you'll be able to make a deal. Adelaide, you haven't killed anyone yet."

"No, she hasn't. And that's a problem."

Cat's heart sank as she saw Jessica Atwell step into view on the landing below them.

"Jessica," Adelaide breathed.

"Put the gun down Adelaide and move over next to Ms. McGuire." As Adelaide jerkily followed her instructions, Jessica moved quickly up the stairs. Her cold and clipped tones were a sharp right turn from the voice she used on TV. "I can't trust you to do anything. You don't even have the doll yet."

When Jessica reached the landing, Cat finally saw her gun with its businesslike silencer on the end. Jessica pointed it in Cat's direction. "I'm pressed for time, Ms. McGuire, and

Adelaide, I'm not in the mood for a chat. Put the bag ⸺e floor and shove it toward me."

⸺at held on to the doll. Then she heard a noise behind her.

"Drop the gun, Ms. Atwell."

Dino. Then as if she were viewing a film in slow motion, Cat saw Jessica look beyond her and shift the barrel of the gun.

"No." Cat acted out of blind instinct, hurling the bag, then leaping after it to push Jessica off balance. Cat saw the flash of fire, heard the deafening sound of the gunshot. Then she and Jessica tumbled head over heels down the flight of stairs. Pain sang up her elbow, then her shoulder. But it was her head that took the worst hit. She saw swirling stars before Jase pulled the woman off of her and Dino sank to his knees beside her.

"You all right?" Dino asked.

"What took you so long?"

He pulled her into his arms and she held on for a long time.

DINO LEANED AGAINST THE WALL in one of the Alsation Towers' executive offices. Jack Phillips stood to his left and Jase flanked him on the right while Cat sat on a carved oak desk and fielded a barrage of questions from her family.

She looked only a little worse for wear, Dino thought. The hotel doctor, a young Asian woman, had checked Cat out, bandaged her elbow, and pronounced that her patient was going to have a stiff leg, a sore shoulder and a goose egg on her head that wouldn't fade for four or five days.

"Smuggled drugs, terrorists, and the Cheshire Cat is right in the middle of it. It's better than a movie. No wonder you don't want to give up your business and settle down." Lucia Merceri thumped her cane on the floor as she shot an approving look at Dino. "And he's on your side. Seems to me you've got yourself a keeper there."

Then Lucia turned her attention to her son-in-law. "With all this excitement and adventure, I may have to visit New York City more often."

Later, Dino might find time to be amused by the expression on Colonel James McGuire's face. But right now, he couldn't quite summon up a grin. However, Cat's burst of laughter did more than the doctor's diagnosis to begin to untangle the knot of fear in his stomach. She was all right.

It had been a close call. He would never forget the fact that he'd nearly been too late. While he'd silently descended three endless flights of stairs, he'd realized what Cat was trying to do—keep Adelaide focused on her. But he'd also sensed the escalating fear and panic in the older woman. And she'd had that gun aimed directly at Cat. It was a high-risk situation and he'd purposely spoken to attract Jessica Atwell's attention, never expecting that Cat would launch herself at the woman.

Once again the image of Cat hurtling down the stairs replayed itself in his mind. She could have broken her neck. He could have lost her forever.

"Stop beating up on yourself," Jase said. "Your visions are what saved her. She was forewarned, so she had an advantage. And you knew just where to find her."

"Visions?" Jack Phillips asked. "You have visions?"

Dino winced inwardly, but luckily, Jack's cell phone rang.

"Yeah," Jack said. After a moment, a smile lit his face. He pocketed the cell and turned to Jase and Dino. "Good news. Adelaide is singing her heart out and her song is all about Jessica Atwell. She's confessed to hiring the man who knifed me, but denies any responsibility for the attempt on Cat's life. Of course, she's cooperating fully in the hopes of making a deal that will lessen her sentence. Down in Paxco, my team has taken Juan Rivero into custody. So far, Atwell is only talk-

ner lawyers, but now that we've identified her, we'll find
er trail, and Creed is a credible witness."

"What about Atwell's connection to terrorists?" Dino asked.

"The CIA is checking into it. I'm figuring it must date back
to her days as an activist. There was a time when she was very
anti-American and she spent time in Central and South
America. And a Senate run takes money. We'll find the connection." Jack's grin widened. "And with Homeland Security
involved—well, they have a lot more freedom than we do in
questioning a suspect."

Dino's attention was suddenly drawn back to Cat as her
father said, "Little girl, why don't you come home with
Gianna and me tonight? You're not going to want to go back
to your apartment."

"No." Dino strode over to Cat and took her hand. "Cat and
I have plans for the rest of the evening."

James McGuire frowned at him. "She's injured and exhausted. And safe. Your job is over."

"What do you mean 'his job'?" Lucia Merceri asked.

"Yes. What do you mean?" Admiral Maxwell chimed in.

With Cat's hand in his, Dino met each one of their eyes—
McGuire's, his boss's, and Lucia Merceri's. "Colonel
McGuire is talking about the fact that he originally hired me
to protect Cat, to keep her safe until this drug smuggling operation was wrapped up. And he's right, my job is over. But
Cat and I have some unfinished business to take care of. We'll
see you tomorrow."

EVERY BONE IN HER BODY ACHED, and the pretty little Asian
doctor had predicted that it was only going to get worse. So
Cat wasn't particularly thrilled when Dino escorted her out
of the hotel and into the same limo that had brought them to

the Alsatian Towers. She'd been hoping they were headed for the suite they'd dressed in earlier. Leaning back against the leather seat, she watched as he handed the driver money.

When he joined her and the limo pulled out into traffic, she slipped her hand into his. "If you want to have sex with me, I'm game, but you're going to have to do most of the work."

"I don't want to have sex with you." His voice was just as clipped and neutral as it had been when he'd talked to her father in the executive offices.

"Lean back and relax."

Cat tried, but she couldn't. She turned to study him, but he didn't return her gaze. As the limo passed in and out of streetlights, his profile looked very grim. And focused.

I don't want to have sex with you? My job is over. Cat and I have some unfinished business to take care of.

The words replayed themselves in a continuous loop in her mind. The adrenaline that had been fueling her ever since Adelaide Creed had stepped out of that washroom stall was fading fast, but the fear blossoming in its place was more fierce than what she had felt when she'd been looking into the barrel of that gun.

Cat and I have some unfinished business to take care of.

He was going to say goodbye, The realization struck her like a blow to the stomach. His job was over, and he would want to join his family in San Francisco for Christmas.

Turning away from Dino, she stared through the smoky glass of the limo, trying to focus, but all she could see were blurred lights. Was she crying?

Cat swiped at her cheeks and found them damp.

The limo suddenly stopped, and Dino didn't wait for the driver. He pushed the door open, and sprang out. Then he turned back and extended his hand. "We're here."

Cat stepped out into the cold and glanced around quickly at her surroundings. She'd wiped away her tears, but her eyes had evidently filled again because she had to blink fast to bring the lights on the huge Christmas tree into focus. Her heart skipped a beat when she realized the limo had dropped them off at Rockefeller Center.

The wind sweeping between the tall buildings surrounding them was icy, and she couldn't prevent a shiver.

Dino swore softly. "I forgot to stop and get your coat. Here." Slipping out of his dress uniform jacket, he dropped it over her shoulders. Then he dragged her forward through the crowd of milling people.

They were at the railing above the skating rink when he stopped short and turned to face her. "This isn't what I planned. I was going to bring you here tomorrow afternoon— after you'd rested."

Blinking the last of the moisture out of her eyes, Cat took a good look at the man standing in front of her. Gone was the laid-back control that Dino usually projected. In its place was a fury that practically crackled in the air around him.

"But you're not going to be in any shape to come here tomorrow. You're not in any shape to be here tonight. C'mon." He grabbed her arm. "We'll do this in the limo."

Cat dug in her heels as her temper sliced through the little pity party she had been indulging in back in the limo. If he'd brought her here to say goodbye… Well, she'd have something to say about that.

She jerked her arm free of his grip. "I don't care to go back to the limo yet. You told my father we had unfinished business to settle. Let's do it. You're going to tell me that you're going back to San Francisco."

He stared at her then. "No."

She fisted her hands on her hips. "You're not going back to see your family for Christmas or to attend your cousin Theo's wedding?"

"Yes, but that's not—"

"Well, I'm coming with you. Get used to the idea."

FOR THE LIFE OF HIM, Dino couldn't find his voice. He was vaguely aware that the people walking past them were sending them curious glances, but he couldn't take his eyes off of Cat.

She poked a finger into his chest. "I know that our original deal was just sex—"

"And it was a very good deal," he said, capturing one of her hands, then the other.

She raised her chin. "Not good enough, evidently. You said in the limo that you didn't want to have sex with me"

For the first time he looked deep into her eyes, and what he saw there—the same mix of fear and hope that he was feeling—finally made the image of her hurtling down the stairs fade away. "I want more than sex."

"You do?"

He brought one hand to his lips. "A lot more."

She swallowed hard. "Me, too."

"I'd planned on bringing you here tomorrow and taking you skating. I wanted to start over where the fictional story began and make it all real." He lifted her left hand and wiggled the engagement ring off. "You'll have to settle for this."

As Cat stared, he dropped to one knee and held the ring out to her. "Marry me, Cat."

She dropped to her good knee, held out her hand and let him slip the ring back on her finger. "Marry me, Dino." Then she threw her arms around him and held on tight.

Around them the crowd broke into applause. Cat found she

was blinking back tears again, but she managed to whisper, "I can always open a toy store in San Francisco."

"Jase has offered me a job here in Manhattan. He thinks we make a good team."

"We can talk about it later. For now, can we please go back to the limo and make love? Come toy with me, Dino."

"I thought you'd never ask." Laughing, he drew her to her feet, scooped her into his arms, and carried her to the waiting limo. The crowd cheered them as they went.

Epilogue

DINO HANDED CAT A frothy glass of champagne, then leaned close to her ear, pitching his voice so that he could be heard above the music and the din of the conversations going on around them. "What do you think of my family's restaurant?"

"It's amazing."

"I've always thought so." Dino let his gaze sweep the room. The Poseidon was aglow with Christmas lights and filled with flowers for Theo's and Sadie's wedding reception. The tables in the main dining room on the lower level had been shoved to the back wall and were now laden with a wide array of Greek and Italian food. His uncle Spiro and Helena were inspecting the spread and giving last-minute instructions to the wait staff. Chairs had been clustered in corners and along the other walls. Some of the guests were crowded around the bar area, others were dancing, and still more had spilled out onto the terrace. Waiters moved among them with trays of champagne and hors d'oeuvres.

Dino turned his gaze back to Cat. "I wanted to see you here."

Cat met his eyes and smiled. "And now that you have?"

He took her free hand and raised it to his lips. "You fit. Perfectly. Now, tell me what you think of my family?"

"They're amazing, too. But I'm still a bit nervous." Cat touched her glass to his, then sipped the icy liquid. "There are a lot of people to keep straight."

Their trip to San Francisco had been delayed, first because the FBI and the CIA had both wanted to question her, and then because of the Christmas day arrival of Lucy's baby, little Merry. They'd both wanted to visit the hospital to greet the new arrival to the family before they left. When they'd finally arrived late last night, the wedding preparations had been in full swing, and she'd only had the briefest of introductions to his family.

"I'm in total sympathy with you on that. My family has doubled in size since the last time I was here. I'm still trying to sort them out myself."

Cat met his eyes and voiced the worry that had been plaguing her ever since she'd stood between Cass and Dino in the church and witnessed the brief but lovely wedding ceremony. "Are you regretting your decision to work with Jase and stay in New York? Because if you are—"

Dino cut her off by placing his fingers on her lips. "I'm not regretting my decision to settle in New York at all. We'll visit my family often. I don't ever intend to be as disconnected from them as I was during my two years working special ops. And who knows, you may eventually decide to expand your business and open a Cheshire Cat in San Francisco." Then removing his fingers, he leaned down and brushed his lips over hers.

Cat felt a little knot of tension unravel. She was considering the feasibility of opening a store in San Francisco. Then she narrowed her eyes, studying him more closely. "Have you had one of your feelings about that?"

He laughed. "No. But my mother mentioned the possibility. And she's the one with the real powers in the family."

He gestured with his glass to the upper level of the restaurant where the bridal party was having pictures taken. "I'll help you out with my cousins' names if you'll refresh mind about the women."

"You're on." Cat studied the line of people the photographe was working with. The bridesmaids wore dresses in pastel hues of blue, pink, lilac and sea-foam green. Each one of the men was so tall, dark and handsome that it almost hurt her eyes to look at them.

"Theo's the one with the bride on his arm," Dino began.

"Thanks." As Cat smiled, the rest of her tension eased. "And the bride's name is Sadie. Those two I'm pretty sure of. And I think I have Nik and Kit figured out. Kit's taller and he's almost always smiling. Nik usually has a serious expression on his face and he's quieter."

"Probably because he's a cop. I like his new wife, J.C. She seems to complement him quite nicely."

Cat shifted her gaze to the short redhead in the green dress. J.C. was easy to remember because she had a very outgoing personality and hardly ever stopped talking. "I like her, too. Now, using the process of elimination, I think the tall blonde is Drew. She designed Sadie's wedding dress and the bridesmaids' dresses, and she goes with Kit."

"She goes very well with Kit indeed," Dino agreed.

"And the very pretty woman with the short dark hair is your cousin Philly. But then I'm stumped," Cat said. "I know that the other tall, dark and handsome man is Philly's new fiancé, but his name escapes me."

"He's Roman Oliver."

Cat turned to find that Dino's mother and a tall man she recalled talking to Cass in the vestibule of the church had joined them.

"And the other couple in the wedding party are Sadie's sister Juliana and her fiancé, Paulo Carlucci," the man continued.

ass cleared her throat. "Cat and Dino, I'd like you to et Mason Leone. He's worked security for the Oliver mily for years."

Mason Leone shook Cat's hand first. She found his grip firm, and she sensed a quiet intensity about him that was not unlike Dino's.

When he gripped Dino's hand, Mason said, "I'd like to have a word with you in private."

Dino said nothing as he led the way to a hallway that ran off the dining room.

"Wish me luck," Cass murmured to Cat in a low voice.

As she turned to face Dino's mother, she noted that the color had risen in Cass's cheeks. "Is something wrong?"

Cass shifted her gaze to meet Cat's for a moment before she looked back at the two men. "I hope not. I'm just a bit nervous. I've been seeing Mason for several months now. He's very old-fashioned in many ways and I think he's going to ask Dino's blessing to ask me to marry him."

Cat glanced back at the two men. They were both standing rather stiffly as if they were taking each other's measure. She slipped her hand into Cass's. "Don't you know what Dino's answer will be?"

Cass shook her head. "My powers don't seem to work where Mason is concerned. I didn't even know I was in love with him for a while. With Dino's father, I knew the moment I saw him."

"That's exactly the way I felt with Dino." Then curious, Cat asked, "What will you do if Dino doesn't give his blessing?"

Cass glanced at her with a smile. "I suppose I'll just have to take matters into my own hands and propose to Mason."

"Good. That was my plan with Dino, but he beat me to it."

Cass raised their joined hands and looked at Cat's engagement ring. "It looks right on you."

"It feels right." The two women looked back at their me
in time to see them move to the bar. A moment later, a bar
tender put two beers in front of them. Lifting his bottle, Dino
tapped it against Mason's before they drank.

."I think it's going well," Cat said.

Still, she noted that Cass didn't completely relax until Dino
and Mason returned. Then her throat tightened as she watched
Dino hug his mother and place her hand in Mason Leone's.

LATER, CASS STOOD on the entrance level of the restaurant with
Mason at her side and watched her family on the dance floor
below. The band was playing a waltz. It had been nearly a year
since the weekend when everything had started. Now her
sister's children and her son were each dancing with the
person the Fates had meant them to be with. Because each of
them had said yes to what the Fates had offered them.

Just as she had said yes. She glanced down at the bright
new engagement ring that Mason had just put on her hand.

"Dino has invited us to visit him in New York," Mason said.
"He wants me to meet his friend Jase. He claims that his old
navy buddy has top-of-the-line security gadgets that he thinks
I might be interested in."

Cass glanced up at him "You're trying to make me feel
better because Dino won't be returning to live in San Francisco." ·

He smiled at her. "It's going to be hard being married to a
woman who sees right through me."

Downstairs, the music changed to something that reminded
Cass of Greece. Spiro led Helena to the center of the floor.
Two by two, the rest of her family followed until they formed
a large circle. For a moment, she and Mason watched as Spiro
led them into a traditional Greek dance. Roman, Sadie and Cat
were a little hesitant, but their partners guided them.

"Shall we join them, Cassandra?" Mason asked.

Cass looked up into her new fiancé's eyes and in that moment, she knew. Along with her children, she had been right to choose what the Fates had offered.

* * * * *

Silhouette Desire kicks off 2009 with
MAN OF THE MONTH, *a yearlong program*
featuring incredible heroes by stellar authors.

When navy SEAL Hunter Cabot returns home for some
much-needed R and R, he discovers he's a married man.
There's just one problem: he's never met his "bride."

Enjoy this sneak peek at Maureen Child's
AN OFFICER AND A MILLIONAIRE.
Available January 2009 from Silhouette Desire.

One

Hunter Cabot, Navy SEAL, had a healing bullet wound in his side, thirty days' leave and, apparently, a wife he'd never met.

On the drive into his hometown of Springville, California, he stopped for gas at Charlie Evans's service station. That's where the trouble started.

"Hunter! Man, it's good to see you! Margie didn't tell us you were coming home."

"Margie?" Hunter leaned back against the front fender of his black pickup truck and winced as his side gave a small twinge of pain. Silently then, he watched as the man he'd known since high school filled his tank.

Charlie grinned, shook his head and pumped gas. "Guess your wife was lookin' for a little 'alone' time with you, huh?"

"My—" Hunter couldn't even say the word. *Wife?* He didn't have a wife. "Look, Charlie..."

"Don't blame her, of course," his friend said with a wink as he finished up and put the gas cap back on. "You being gone all the time with the SEALs must be hard on the ol' love life."

He'd never had any complaints, Hunter thought, frowning at the man still talking a mile a minute. "What're you—"

"Bet Margie's anxious to see you. She told us all about that R and R trip you two took to Bali." Charlie's dark brown eyebrows lifted and wiggled.

"Charlie..."

"Hey, it's okay, you don't have to say a thing, man."

What the hell could he say? Hunter shook his head, paid for his gas and as he left, told himself Charlie was just losing it. Maybe the guy had been smelling gas fumes too long.

But as it turned out, it wasn't just Charlie. Stopped at a red light on Main Street, Hunter glanced out his window to smile at Mrs. Harker, his second-grade teacher who was now at least a hundred years old. In the middle of the crosswalk, the old lady stopped and shouted, "Hunter Cabot, you've got yourself a wonderful wife. I hope you appreciate her."

Scowling now, he only nodded at the old woman—the only teacher who'd ever scared the crap out of him. What the hell was going on here? Was everyone but him nuts?

His temper beginning to boil, he put up with a few more comments about his "wife" on the drive through town before finally pulling into the wide, circular drive leading to the Cabot mansion. Hunter didn't have a clue what was going on, but he planned to get to the bottom of it. Fast.

He grabbed his duffel bag, stalked into the house and paid no attention to the housekeeper, who ran at him, fluttering both hands. "Mr. Hunter!"

"Sorry, Sophie," he called out over his shoulder as he took the stairs two at a time. "Need a shower, then we'll talk."

He marched down the long, carpeted hallway to the rooms that were always kept ready for him. In his suite, Hunter tossed the duffel down and stopped dead. The shower in his bathroom was running. His *wife?*

Anger and curiosity boiled in his gut, creating a churning mass that had him moving forward without even thinking about it. He opened the bathroom door to a wall of steam and the sound of a woman singing—off-key. Margie, no doubt.

Well, if she was his wife… Hunter walked across the room, yanked the shower door open and stared in at a curvy, naked, temptingly wet woman.

She whirled to face him, slapping her arms across her naked body while she gave a short, terrified scream.

Hunter smiled. "Hi, honey. I'm home."

* * * * *

Be sure to look for
AN OFFICER AND A MILLIONAIRE
by USA TODAY *bestselling author Maureen Child.*
Available January 2009 from Silhouette Desire.

CELEBRATE
60 YEARS
OF PURE READING PLEASURE
WITH **HARLEQUIN**®!

We'll be spotlighting a different series
every month throughout 2009
to celebrate our 60th anniversary.
Look for Silhouette Desire® in January!

Collect all 12 books in the Silhouette Desire®
Man of the Month continuity, starting in
January 2009 with *An Officer and a Millionaire*
by *USA TODAY* bestselling author
Maureen Child.

*Look for one new Man of the Month title
every month in 2009!*

REQUEST YOUR FREE BOOKS!

2 FREE NOVELS PLUS 2 FREE GIFTS!

HARLEQUIN®

Blaze™

Red-hot reads!

HB08R

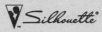

COMING NEXT MONTH

#441 EVERY BREATH YOU TAKE... Hope Tarr
Undercover FBI agent Cole Whittaker never has trouble putting his life on the line...but his heart? He almost lost it once, five years ago, and he's not chancing it again. Until he takes on a security job—to guard the one woman he's never been able to forget...

#442 LONE STAR SURRENDER Lisa Renee Jones
Rebellious undercover agent Constantine Vega takes D.A. Nicole Ward on the sexiest ride of her life as he protects her from a vengeful enemy—but who will protect her from him?

#443 NAKED AMBITION Jule McBride
J. D. Johnson's ambition is twofold: reclaim the life that once fed his soul as a successful country musician, and win back his small-town Southern belle. Only, Susannah's been kicking up her heels in NYC. Good thing J.D. knows all the right moves....

#444 NO HOLDING BACK Isabel Sharpe
24 Hours: Lost, Bk. 2
Reporter Hannah O'Reilly will do most anything for a story—including gate-crashing reclusive millionaire Jack Battle's estate on a stormy New Year's Eve. But as the snow piles up and sexy Jack starts making his moves, Hannah is achingly aware there's no holding back....

#445 A FEW GOOD MEN Tori Carrington
Uniformly Hot!/Encounters
Four soldiers, four destinies, four complete short stories! While on a tour of duty, Eric, Matt, Eddie and Brian have become a family. Only now, on their way home from Iraq, they have no idea what—or *who*—awaits them....

#446 AFTER DARK Wendy Etherington
"Irresistible" is how Sloan Caldwell describes Aidan Kendrick. The reclusive millionaire mogul may seem a lone wolf, but Sloan's sirenlike sensuality will soon change his ways....

www.eHarlequin.com